LEGEND

OF THE

FAIRY CROSS

Enjoy!
C. C. Archambeault

by *M. Archambeault*

C. C. Archambeault
and
M. Archambeault

Legend of the Fairy Cross

This book is a work of fiction but based on events described in
the Holy Bible.

Printed in the United States of America through
CreateSpace Independent Publishing Platform.
First Paperback Edition: April, 2017

BISAC:
Juvenile Fiction: Religious: Christian: Action & Adventure

If you would like to read more from C. C. Archambeault,
please visit author's website: ccarchambeault.com

ISBN-13: 978-1545014783

ISBN-10: 1545014787

042217

Dedications

To my Grandparents, Mary and Jim Cole,
who gave me my first Fairy Stone Cross
when I was a child and told me the
Legend of the Fairy Stone Cross.

and

To my best friend, Viktoriya,
I thank Jesus for bringing you into my life.
You and Daniel are true blessings.

Table of Contents

(Table of Contents continued on next page.)

(Table of Contents continued.)

Chapter 1

The Bear

"Go on, I dare you!" taunted one of the boys.

"Yeah!" the other boys joined in. "Go on, Dustu, ride him!" Sitting safely on a high branch of a tree, the boys fluttered their wings in eager anticipation.

From his perch in the tree, Dustu looked down at the brown bear who was near a patch of berry bushes. He didn't really want to ride the bear, but his friends had dared him. If he didn't try, his friends would think he was a coward. So, he took a deep breath and spread his wings. He scooted off the branch and floated quietly down to the ground. He hunched down and began sneaking toward the unsuspecting bear.

The bear, busily enjoying eating the ripe berries, did not notice the small boy who was creeping low in the tall grass and silently moving toward him. Suddenly the bear felt something on his back! He reared up and backward, throwing the thing off him. He turned with a roar. Seeing the boy, he snarled, "What are you doing, brat! How dare you jump on me!"

Stunned, Dustu lay on the ground. His wing was hurt, but he ignored it and immediately jumped up.

"Answer me!" the bear roared.

But instead of answering, fear swept over Dustu, so he ran to the nearest tree and climbed up as fast and high as he could. Unfortunately, it wasn't a very tall tree … or very strong. The bear quickly followed him and stood up, putting his mighty front paws on the thin trunk of the swaying tree. Dustu fearfully clung to the branch with all his strength.

*

Awinita looked up from gathering wild-rose petals as several boys frantically flew by her. She recognized them as her young brother's friends. She quickly looked around, but did not see Dustu. "Where's Dustu?" she hollered after the fleeing boys.

"Bear!" one of them called back to her as he continued flying away.

Oh, no, she thought, *what have they been up too?* She dropped her basket and ran in the direction from where the boys were escaping. She heard growling and then she saw the bear. He was standing on his hind legs, reaching up into a small tree. He was swiping his paws up toward Dustu's feet, as they dangled from the highest branch.

"What's going on here?" she called to them in the spirit language that all creatures of the forest use to communicate with each other.

The bear turned and dropped his front paws to the ground. "Is he one of yours?" Without waiting for a reply, the bear growled, "This kid jumped on my back. He actually had the nerve to try to ride *me*!"

"Oh, sir, I'm so sorry. He should be ashamed for doing that." She looked up into the tree and saw Dustu's frightened wide-eyes. "What's wrong with you, Dustu? Apologize to him!"

Dustu's voice trembled as the lowered his eyes and thought to the bear, "I'm sorry sir. It was a stupid thing to do. My friends dared me to ride you, and I ..."

"You did this on a *dare*?" Awinita interrupted, incredulous. "A stupid DARE? Do you have to do every dumb thing that some idiot dares you to? When are you going to think for yourself?"

Dustu hung his head in shame.

Awinita turned and thought to the angry bear, "This will never happen again, sir. I hope you will accept my brother's apology."

"All right," the bear muttered as he began to saunter off. "Just keep on eye on him. Next time, I won't be so forgiving."

Dustu climbed down out of the tree with his left wing drooping downward.

"You've hurt yourself, haven't you?" Awinita asked impatiently.

Dustu nodded.

"OK, come here." Awinita gently lifted the injured wing and closed her eyes. As she held his limp wing, she felt the warm healing energy flow from her hands into Dustu's wing.

Dustu sighed with relief and whispered gratefully, "Oh, it does feel so much better now."

Awinita continued to hold his wing for a few seconds more. "There," she said, "it should be fine now. You're lucky that you weren't hurt more seriously or I wouldn't have been able to help."

"Thanks," he said as he carefully fluttered his healed wing. He paused and asked, "How come only girls can heal and boys can't?"

Awinita smiled down at him and answered jokingly, "Because females eventually become mothers of accident-prone boys who always need healing, that's why."

"So, what gifts do men have?"

"Men have the gift of extra strength," she answered. "Just look at Waya. He's really strong, isn't he? He can lift four times his own weight!"

"I want to be as strong as Waya, too," Dustu said eagerly, looking up at her. "Do you think I will be?"

"I don't know," Awinita grinned, "If you don't stop doing stupid things, you may not live to be ten."

"What's all the commotion about?" a deep voice called out.

Awinita and Dustu turned toward the voice. "Is that you, Adahy?" Awinita called out.

A handsome young man with large powerful wings appeared out of the forest greenery. "Of course," Adahy smiled. Looking at Awinita kneeling in the grass next to Dustu with her wings lowered, he knew she had used her healing touch and would need some rosehips to get her strength back. Without a word, Adahy reached into the pouch hanging from his waist. Dropping down to kneel next to her, he took her hand and filled it with several round red rosehips.

"Thank you," she blushed. "How did you ...?"

With a knowing smile, Adahy interrupted, "All the years we've been in the forest together—with you healing every creature who crosses your path—I think I know you well enough by now. Why do you think I always carry extra rosehips? Now, what's all the fuss about?"

Awinita sighed and answered, "Dustu was dared by his friends to ride a bear, and the bear didn't want any part of it."

Adahy frowned and shook his head at Dustu. "I don't blame him—the bear, I mean." He looked at the boy and said mockingly, "A dare, huh? How about I dare you to gather extra firewood for the village? Would you take that dare? Would you? C'mon, don't be a chicken ... I double dare you!"

Dustu grinned and shook his head.

"So," Adahy playfully flicked Dustu's pointed ear. "You *can* say no to a dare, can't you?"

"Yeah, I guess I can," Dustu giggled.

4

*

The three of them walked back to the wild-rose thicket so Awinita could retrieve her basket. "Do you need some help gathering?" Adahy asked.

"Thank you," Awinita smiled at him. "Just a few more rose hips if you can find them. I had to heal Dustu's wing—as you have guessed—and I want to give some to the Medicine Woman."

"So, are your healing abilities getting even stronger?" Adahy asked.

"Yes, the Medicine Woman says my healing gift is growing quite fast—for my age," she answered.

"Well, you're seventeen years old now, so in one more year you should know how strong it'll finally be. I think the Medicine Woman will want to train you to take her place one day … then just think how all the men will want you for their wife," he teased.

Awinita drew her damaged wing behind her back, trying to conceal the missing half. She wondered why he would say such a thing knowing no man could possibly want her with her wing the way it was. She quickly turned away before he could see the tears forming in her eyes, and reached over to gather her basket.

Realizing he had caused her pain with his teasing, Adahy put his hand on hers. "I'm sorry, I didn't mean to upset you. I just thought that you might be considering … your future. Soon you'll be old enough to marry, you know."

Looking away, Awinita said softly, "Things are different now … I'm different now."

Adahy gently turned her face towards him. "Nothing has changed, Awinita. You are still the same fairy you've always been. Please believe me." Quickly Adahy changed the subject. He turned to Dustu, "So, kid, hurt your wing, did you? So how is it now?" Adahy asked as he fluttered his strong wings and rose up into the air.

5

"It's OK now; no big deal," Dustu replied, and then he too fluttered his wings and rose up beside Adahy.

Awinita was still irritated with her young brother. "Not a big deal? You could have been severely hurt. What do you think Waya would say about this? I know how much you admire him and want to be like him when you grow up. You know he would tell you to respect the animals who share the forest with us, not tease them," she scolded.

An older man suddenly appeared from behind the trees, "Did someone say my name?"

Both Dustu and Adahy landed softly on the ground. "Waya!" Dustu exclaimed as he ran toward him.

"Hi, Waya," Adahy greeted, "we didn't hear you come up."

"Of course not, that's why Waya is the best hunter and tracker in the village!" Dustu exclaimed as he looked admiringly up at Waya.

"I was looking for all of you," Waya said as he hugged Dustu. "I just had an interesting conversation with a grouchy brown bear ... anyone know anything about that?"

Dustu just groaned and hung his head.

Waya looked down at Dustu. "Don't worry, boy. When we are young, we all sometimes do crazy and stupid things. What's important is that we *learn* from those mistakes and not repeat them." Waya turned to Awinita and Adahy. "Like I said, I was looking for you. We need to get back to the village. We have visitors."

"Visitors? Who are they? Where are they from?" Dustu eagerly pestered Waya.

Waya tried to shush Dustu, "Just wait; you'll see soon enough."

*

As they went back through the forest to their village, Waya and Dustu walked ahead, with Awinita and Adahy walking slowly behind them. "Do you still have nightmares about the great fire?" Adahy asked softly.

Awinita looked down with sadness, "Yes, I can't help it. I have one nearly every night. I don't know if I'll ever be able to sleep without those terrible dreams."

Adahy took her delicate hand and placed a piece of deep-pink rose quartz in it. "I found this in the river. I've heard that it helps soothe troubled sleep, so I thought you might like it."

Awinita held the cool, smooth stone in her hand. She gazed at its beauty and then looked up into Adahy's handsome face. "Oh, thank you!" she said, smiling widely. "This is so kind of you!"

Happy to see Awinita's face light up again, he smiled back, "Anything for you."

Chapter 2

Visitors

The village was in a tizzy. "We have visitors!" several fairies whispered excitedly to them as they entered and crossed the clearing to the village huts. Awinita and Dustu parted with Waya and Adahy, and walked to their hut where they lived with their mother and baby sister.

"We have visitors from very far away!" their mother greeted them as they entered the small home. "There'll be a feast tonight and then we'll hear what the travelers have to say."

"That's exciting," Awinita said happily. "I gathered some things ... here are rose petals and we found some rose hips. I need to eat a few, but I'll take the rest to the Medicine Woman."

"Wonderful," her mother said, smiling. "I'll prepare the rose petals for tonight." She watched as her daughter removed the least perfect red rosehips for herself, leaving the best ones to give to the Medicine Woman. She thought to herself, *Awinita is such a kind and thoughtful girl. She always wants to give the best of what she has to others.* The fact that Awinita needed to eat extra rosehips told her that her daughter had used her healing abilities on someone ... most likely her brother. She sighed. *That boy. He's always into trouble.* She shrugged her shoulders. She knew Awinita would not "tattle-tale" on her brother by telling what had happened—unless it was necessary—so she put it out of her mind.

*

After a little while, Awinita wrapped up the bright red rosehips and took them to the Medicine Woman. As she entered the Medicine Woman's hut, she breathed in the aroma of herbs and spices that filled the air. All along the walls and hanging from the ceiling were all kinds of plants and roots—in various stages of drying. Aside from the forest, this was her favorite place to be.

"Hello, dear," the elderly woman greeted her. Awinita smiled and handed her the bag of rosehips. "Oh, thank you," the Medicine Woman said as she gratefully took them and placed them into a woven-grass bowl. "Where's Adahy?"

Surprised, Awinita replied, "I don't know."

The Medicine Woman knowingly smiled. "OK, it's just that he seems to be close by ... wherever you are, that is, especially since the fire." Awinita blushed as the old woman continued, "He likes you very much, you know. I remember when you two were little imps. You and he would be the last to come in from the forest for dinner. You, always looking for any hurt critter to heal, and Adahy, making sure you never lost your way."

"Yes, Father would always have to call us in." Awinita smiled as she remembered meeting her dad at the edge—where the village met the forest. He would always laugh and say, "You'd think the fireflies would remind you of suppertime!" Her heart flooded with longing and loss at the memories of her father. She quickly changed her thoughts back to what the Medicine Woman was saying about Adahy and her. "He's just nice to everyone," Awinita shrugged.

"Yes he is, but *you* are special to him."

Awinita just looked at the elderly woman. "Why would I be special? The great fire burned one of my wings half off. Adahy is twenty years old and could have *any* girl in the village, so why would he want a seventeen year-old with a bum wing?" Then she murmured, "I'll never be beautiful ... or fly and work like the other fairies do."

The Medicine Woman smiled and shook her head at Awinita, "Oh, but you *are* beautiful, my dear. Beauty comes from the inside, not just what's on the outside. Do you see my scar?" The Medicine Woman lifted back her wing, pulled up her sleeve, and held out her arm—showing a long ragged scar. "Does this make me ugly? Do you think less of me because an injured and frightened raccoon accidentally did this?"

Shocked, Awinita gasped, "No, Medicine Woman, of course not!"

"As for your ability to work ... just look at the wonderful rosehips that you have brought me. I can always count on you for the best quality." The kind woman then gently took Awinita's sweet face in her hands and said softly, "So my dear, you were beautiful and hardworking before the fire. Now you are beautiful and hardworking after it ... and you always will be. We all see your beauty and character ... and so does Adahy."

* * *

After everyone had eaten, the whole village sat around the fire-pit, waiting for the visiting fairies to speak. There were four of them sitting there. They were older and their clothes were worn from travel, but they had a youthful energy—and eyes that had an unusual brightness and warmth in them. Then one stood and began to speak. "We are from a faraway land, from across the great sea. We have been traveling for many years, telling all the fairies of a great and marvelous event." He paused, took a deep breath and announced, "The prophecy has been fulfilled. The Savior of the world has been born."

All of the village fairies gasped. Everyone knew of the ancient prophecy. It had been passed down through all the generations through the "Keeper of the Legends." Awinita's father had been their village Keeper.

"He is of the human people, not of the fairies," the visitor continued. "He was born in a small town far away ... but I'm getting ahead of myself, so let me start at the beginning." He took another deep breath and began again, "We knew of the ancient prophecy, of course, but when we saw the star—the large and amazingly bright star in the sky, we knew it was time. We got word of a caravan that was following the bright star, so we joined it ... but naturally we remained invisible to the humans. It was a long and tiring journey, so we rode on their camels—with the camel's permission, of course.

"After many days, the caravan arrived at a small town called Bethlehem, and following the light of the star, we found the Child and His parents in a stable. There were great beings of light—with wings much greater than our own—standing around the Baby. They called themselves 'Angels.' Since the humans couldn't see us but the Angels could, we were able to go right up to the Baby. Imagine our surprise when we realized that *He* could see us! The Angels told us His name is Jesus. So we played with Him and even made Him smile!

"We stayed with Him for a number of years while He and His parents journeyed to Egypt, and then back to their home village of Nazareth. We wanted to continue to help protect Him, but the

Angels came to us and told us we needed to go and tell all the fairies in the world that the Savior has come.

"Many years have passed as we journeyed through all the lands, telling everyone the great news. When the time came for us to cross the great sea, we returned to Nazareth to ask the parents of Jesus, Mary and her husband Joseph, to help us construct a boat that could carry us across it."

Dustu interrupted, "You let them see you?"

"Yes," the visitor continued. "We had to. We knew they would keep our existence a secret. Then Joseph, being a very skilled carpenter, traveled with us to the edge of the sea. He and a friend made a boat with the same proportions—but smaller—of another boat that had survived the seas many years ago. It was a boat that saved a man named Noah and his family from the great flood. Everyone called it 'Noah's Ark.' So then, with the help of the sea creatures, we traveled across the great water to this land so that we could continue our mission.

"It has been over 30 years since we first saw the infant Savior, so He most certainly has started His ministry by now." He paused and looked around, "Are there any questions?"

The questions and answers continued throughout the evening. Many of the children were tired, so after several hours, everyone retired to their huts to sleep. But, instead of dreaming of the miraculous news, Awinita dreamed of the great fire—again.

Chapter 3

Fiery Dreams

Awinita tossed and turned in her bed as she dreamed.

It started out as a normal hot summer's day, and most of the village was out gathering food. Adahy and some other young men were fishing in the river. Dustu and his friends were searching the trees for nuts. Waya and some of the older men were off hunting. Awinita and the other teenage girls were gathering greens. Everyone was spread throughout the woods, cheerfully busy with their tasks. Awinita could hear Waya's wife singing in the distance as she gathered dandelions. Because the sun was still shining so brightly, no one noticed the angry dark clouds that had quickly formed overhead to the west.

Suddenly there was a deafening sound—a terrible crash. Everyone looked up, but could see nothing unusual. Then the forest animals began running by. "What's wrong?" Awinita thought to them.

"Lightening!" a panicked deer thought back as she bounded past. "Fire!"

"Fire!" Awinita shouted out. "The deer said there is fire!"

Awinita looked about, but saw no fire. But then some of the villagers began to smell smoke, and panic spread. They gathered what they had and flew toward the river. Then Awinita smelled the smoke. She quickly looked all around. "Dustu!" she shouted anxiously. "Where are you?"

The boy crashed through the dry brush. "Here!" Dustu coughed to her, gasping for breath. "Fire in the woods!" he coughed again, while carefully cradling two baby chicks in his arms.

"Run and fly over the river!" Awinita shouted. "Where's Father?"

Dustu nodded back to where the smoke was gathering, "He and the others were over there, last time I saw them!"

"Go on!" Awinita frantically shoved him in the direction of the river, and then looked toward the thickening smoke. She knew that she should also run toward the river and fly across to safety, but her father and many others were still out there. She began to run sideways around the oncoming cloud of smoke, trying to see beyond it. The wind was picking up. The smoke was quickly becoming thicker. She coughed as it blew toward her and burned in her throat. *How could this happen so fast?* She thought to herself. *What should I do?* Then she saw the flames. They were racing toward her! Before she knew it, flames were all around her! She was momentarily frozen in shock at her immediate danger.

"Run!" a voice yelled from a distance.

Jolted out of her horror, she turned and ran. She felt the intense heat and her eyes began to sting. There were tiny sparkles of fire swirling in the air. The smoke was so thick now—she could hardly see. Coughing violently, she tried to catch a breath.

"Here!" the voice called, sounding nearer.

She stumbled and fell, then got up, spread her wings, and began to fly. She barely cleared the ground when crippling pain shot through her wing. She screamed in agony and fell to the ground. Suddenly powerful arms were around her, crushing her, smothering her burning wing. "Adahy," she whispered before she passed out from the pain.

*

Awinita woke with tears in her eyes and her body soaked with sweat. She lay there in the darkness, remembering. Remembering the haze of smoke and pain. Remembering how she had opened her eyes to see real fear in Adahy's face as he carried her in his strong arms to safety. Remembering how he plunged them both into the cold river, easing her burning pain. Remembering how the rain started, saving the rest of the forest and their village.

Tears ran down her cheeks. Remembering the many they lost that awful day: Waya's wife, Adahy's father, and worst of all, her own father. She reached around to her ragged wing and ran her fingers along the burned edge. Her heart sank, remembering that she will never fly like the others—ever again.

She tried to turn her thoughts to something good. She smiled gently, remembering the two baby chicks in Dustu's arms. As he had run from the fire, he had seen a terrified mother owl on the ground with her two babies. The fire was fast approaching, but she wouldn't leave her little ones. So Dustu flew over a patch of burning brush, scooped up the chicks, and escaped the flames with the grateful mother owl flying closely behind him.

She sighed and turned over to try and get some more sleep.

Chapter 4

Decisions and Preparations

The visitors stayed in the village for several days until they felt rested enough to continue on their long journey. The Savior had finally come, and certainly His ministry was being heard by all ... except by the fairies in *this* land, far across the vast sea. The elders of their village felt that they should do something about this. They should send a small group to go and find the Savior, listen to Him, and then return to tell everyone what they had seen and heard. They all agreed to the plan, but who would they send? Many names were suggested, but Waya's name was the one most favored to go ... and to lead.

A village meeting was called. All the fairies gathered at the center of the village. Awinita, Dustu, and their mother (holding the baby) sat with Waya and Adahy. When the discussion of the plan began, the elder's didn't even have to mention Waya's name because he was the first to volunteer. He said it would be a long and dangerous journey, and since he had no family (he had lost his childless wife in the great fire) he was a logical choice. Others began to volunteer as well, including Adahy. He was chosen because he was young and very strong, plus he had an uncanny ability for sensing direction—a necessary gift for a journey such as this.

Awinita listened as the elders agreed that Waya and Adahy were two good choices for the important journey. She remembered how her father had always felt and hoped that this event would occur during his lifetime, and how he would want to meet the Savior. Suddenly she was overcome with the feeling that *she* should be the one to go in his place. To her mother's horror, Awinita raised her hand. "I would like to volunteer to go. My father, a Keeper of the Legends as you all know, had always told us the story of the coming Savior. He would have insisted on going, but since he is no longer with us, I should go in his place. I know I'm only seventeen, but I should go ... to honor my father."

The elders turned to Awinita's mother who was still in shock. "She is your eldest daughter; we cannot approve this without your permission."

Awinita turned to her mother, "Please, Mom, I need to go. I have to go. Dustu can help you. He can gather firewood, berries, and nuts. I'm sure the village will help you with anything you need. Please. I'll be back as soon as I can," she pleaded. "Please."

Awinita's mother was surprised to see Awinita so insistent. This was the first time since the fire that she had seen her daughter so excited. The loss of her father and the constant nightmares had not let her move forward and heal. But, she knew it would be a long and dangerous trip. "You're only seventeen years old; how can I say yes to this?" her mother said, shaking her head.

"I won't be alone, Waya and Adahy will be with me!" Awinita pleaded.

Her mother thought for a moment. She knew Waya looked upon Awinita and Dustu as if they were his own children, and would look after her. She also knew that Adahy had loved her daughter since they were children together, and would give his life for her—and almost did during the great fire. She remembered how much her husband had wanted this day to come. She knew, without a doubt, that he indeed would have volunteered for this journey—he probably would have even led it. She also knew her daughter—her strong will—was so much like her father. She knew ... and so she unhappily finally agreed.

* * *

Preparations had to be made. Provisions would be needed. The word spread throughout the forest, as the fairies told every animal they came across about the upcoming journey. Many of the creatures of the forest wanted to help. The Queen Bee of a nearby hive offered a gift of honey, made from the pollen of the wild-rose. The squirrels hunted for extra nuts. The rabbits brought dandelion leaves and flowers (that they managed not to eat on the way). The birds shook their bodies to let their softest feathers fall to the ground to be gathered. The mice brought seeds from pine cones. The mother owl, whose chicks Dustu had saved from the fire, volunteered to find two deer to carry the group through the forest. Even the grouchy brown bear wanted to help. He brought them a large fish he had caught in the river.

The villagers shelled the nuts and bagged them in woven grass pouches. They dried the flowers and leaves. They smoked the fish. Extra warm cloaks were made from the feathers. Everyone worked swiftly in preparation.

The journey would take many months, and the most dangerous part would be traveling across the great sea. The visitors offered their boat for the group to use, since they would be continuing their mission across the land and would not be coming back. Two magnificent eagles heard about the voyage from the birds. They too wanted to help, so they agreed to go ahead and find the boat hidden at the shore, according to the directions the visitors had given them.

Finally, everything was ready.

Chapter 5

The Journey Begins

The anxiously awaited morning finally arrived. It was very early—the ground was still covered with dew. The entire village was there to say goodbye and to wish the travelers a safe journey. Awinita hugged her tearful mother and her yawning baby sister. "Don't worry, I'll be back," she said smiling, but fighting tears herself. Then she hugged Dustu.

"I want to come," he said sourly, frowning.

"Come on, Dustu, we've been over this before. You're too young and Mom needs your help."

"I'm *not* too young, and the guys said they would help Mom all they could," he retorted. "I should go too."

"Sorry," she sighed as she kissed the top of his head. "Be good."

She picked up her bag and walked to the waiting deer. As she stood next to the deer towering above her she thought to herself, *How am I going to get up there with my damaged wing?*

Suddenly, Adahy was next to her. "Need a lift?" he asked, smiling. "Yes, please," she gratefully answered. As he wrapped his strong arms around her she murmured, "Not even out of the village and I need help."

With one powerful flit of his wings, Adahy flew up and set her on the back of the deer. "You know," Adahy said as he turned to face her, "with your powerful healing touch, you may be the most helpful on our long journey."

She looked into his warm brown eyes. "Thank you," she smiled weakly. Adahy picked up his bag and took his place with Awinita on the deer. Waya rode the second deer. The rest of their supply packs were lifted up to them.

One of the village elders came forward and said, "Safe journey. We will pray for you all."

As they waved goodbye, the deer turned and began to walk toward the east, but staying close to the river. Awinita twisted back to look at her home that soon disappeared behind the forest trees. She quickly brushed away the tear that began to run down her cheek.

The group rode along in silence, hearing only the sounds of the deer hooves walking through the underbrush ... each thinking to themselves. Waya thought of the long journey ahead and the dangers they might face. Adahy thought about the trip as an adventure. But Awinita thought of her mother and the kids ... had she done the right thing to go so far away? And for so long? If something happened to her on this dangerous journey ... and with the loss of her father still so heavy on her mother's heart ... would her mother be OK?

She was lost in her thoughts when she became conscious of how close Adahy was sitting behind her. She knew he couldn't help but be staring at her ugly, crippled, useless wing.

Adahy broke the silence, "Your hair smells nice."

Momentarily surprised that he would be noticing her hair instead of her deformity, she turned and smiled, "I wash it in water with lavender. Remember that chickadee with the hurt foot?"

"Yes, I do. She was so grateful when you helped her that she wouldn't quit singing," Adahy laughed.

"Well, when I went back to that part of the forest, she called me over to tell me about a nice patch of lavender she had found that she thought I might like. So now, whenever I visit there, she greets me and shows me the best patches of herbs and flowers," Awinita explained.

"Chickadees have always been your favorite bird, haven't they?" Adahy asked.

Awinita smiled. "Oh yes, I love that they are always so friendly and helpful."

"And don't forget fearless. They're always the first bird to land on you to say 'hello.'" Adahy paused and then added with a grin, "Anyway, the lavender smells very nice."

"Thanks," she replied, smiling. But then she wondered why he would even notice her hair, or even care. Then she remembered what the Medicine Woman had said—that he found her pretty. *No*, she thought to herself. *He's just being kind because we have been friends since we were children. He couldn't have any interest in me, other than friendship.*

Then she dared to wonder, *but what if the Medicine Woman was right? What if he really is interested in me? What if their friendship is turning into something more? He's so nice, and I have always liked him ... really liked him ... and I hadn't really noticed before how handsome he is ... and how much I like it when he's around ....* Then she chastised herself, *Snap out of it, silly! He could have any girl in the village. I see how they all look at him, hoping that he would ask them to marry. He probably will ask one of them after we get back from this journey ... but why hadn't he asked one of them before? He is certainly of the proper age ... so what is he waiting for?* Then the thought crept back into her mind, *is he waiting for me?* She shook her head to clear the ridiculous idea, but couldn't help notice the warm wave of peace that passed through her heart.

*

Waya's deer—in the lead—thought to Waya, "Oh, here are bushes of our favorite berries! Do you mind if we stop for a while?"

Waya thought back to the deer, "Of course not." Then he said out loud, "Our deer friends need to have lunch, so we might as well eat too."

Waya and Adahy fluttered their wings and slid off the deer backs. Adahy turned to help Awinita down. "I'm sorry to be such a burden," she said as Adahy's strong arms held her as she slid down. "I wish my wings were strong enough."

"Not a problem," Adahy grinned. "I enjoy helping you."

Awinita blushed.

They sat on a log and opened their packs. After lunch, the deer returned and they were on their way again. After hours of travel, the sun disappeared below the forest treetops. Soon their way was nearly engulfed in darkness, with the occasional flicker of fireflies and the chorus of crickets happily chirping away.

"Let's make camp here," Waya announced.

They dismounted and quickly gathered sticks and brush to make a modest hut. Waya and Adahy skillfully bent and twisted sticks together to make the hut framework while Awinita gathered leafy vines to cover the frame. The evening was beginning to get colder, so they cleared a space in the center of the hut and made a small fire. The smoke went up and exited the hut through the center hole at the top. They unrolled and spread their woven grass mats on the ground. They were having a nice leisurely dinner when one of the deer stuck her nose into the hut opening. "I think we've been followed," she thought to them.

"What!" Waya was instantly on alert. "Followed? By who ... or what?"

"It's a young doe," the deer thought. "She's carrying someone, and she's upset because he wants her to go faster."

"How far away are they?" Adahy asked.

"Not far, not far at all," the deer answered. "I'll take you back some so you can see who it is."

"All right, thank you," Waya thought back to the deer. Then he turned to Adahy and Awinita. "I'll go, and you two stay here and guard the camp. I'll be back soon." Before they had time to object, Waya had flown up onto the deer's back and they were gone.

"Who would be following us?" Adahy muttered. "No one at the village put up a fuss that they weren't coming."

Awinita groaned. "I know someone who *did* put up a fuss ... my little brother. But he wouldn't have ... he couldn't have ... it can't be him."

In less than an hour, Waya came riding back on his deer ... with Dustu sitting in front of him.

Chapter 6

Giants

"I'm not going back. If you send me, I'll just ask another deer to take me and I'll follow you again," Dustu frowned as he tightened his wings behind his back and crossed his arms stubbornly.

Awinita covered her face with her hands, and muttered, "What are we going to do with you? You don't listen and you don't obey." She raised her head and looked at the boy. "And what about Mom? She needs your help while I'm gone."

"It's OK. I left her a note, and my friends said they would gather firewood for her and do whatever she needed. They promised," Dustu said defiantly.

"She's going to be sooo upset."

Waya interrupted Awinita's groaning, "We'll have to take him with us. It's not safe to have him continually trying to follow us; he's bound to get into trouble."

"Trouble is his middle name," Adahy added shaking his head.

"All right," Awinita relented. "But you have to obey whatever Waya tells you! Do you understand? Do you?"

"OK, I'll do whatever Waya says," Dustu said happily, "except if he says to go back."

"Hey kid, are you hungry?" Adahy asked.

"No, not very much."

"So you brought some food with you?" Awinita asked suspiciously.

"Of course I did. I'm not stupid, you know," he smirked. "I know how to prepare."

"OK, then, we were about to go to sleep. Where's your sleeping mat?"

Dustu gave her a vacant stare.

"OK, Mr. Prepared, you can share mine with me. Tomorrow morning you're going to find some tall grass and I'll weave you one."

"OK," he said sheepishly.

As they settled down to sleep, Awinita held her brother close. "You're such a brat, you know," she whispered in his ear.

"Yeah, I know," he whispered back. "But I can't help it."

She kissed the top of his head and whispered, "Goodnight."

*

The next morning, after breakfast, they walked to the river bank and filled their water skins while Dustu gathered some long grass. Then they were on their way again. Awinita tucked the grass under her leg and with several pieces, began to weave. After several hours she had made a small mat.

The trek through the woods was slow and tiring, but it wasn't particularly quiet anymore—because of Dustu. He was delighted to be with Waya and he chattered about everything. Since his father had died in the great fire, Dustu had attached himself to Waya. The older man seemed to enjoy the boy, as he had no children of his own. He was an excellent father figure ... he was good for Dustu.

They spent another night in the forest. Dustu tried to be as much help as he could, working quickly and efficiently. They built the hut in record time. It was obvious that the boy wanted the group to be glad that he was with them.

The next morning after breakfast, Dustu gathered the water skins and off he went to the river to fill them. He was filling the last one when he suddenly felt uneasy ... like he was being watched. He quickly looked about and then froze. There standing to the side of him was a girl child, who was five times his size. She was obviously a child of the human people.

"You're a fairy!" she exclaimed in awe, pointing at him.

Dustu instantly made himself invisible.

"No!" she cried out. "Don't go!" she pleaded.

Dustu quickly looked about and saw no one else, so he turned himself visible again.

"Oh! You *are* a fairy! I know you are. I've heard the stories!" she clapped her hands with glee.

"Yes, I am," he said quietly. "Can you please lower your voice? Are there others of your people around?"

"Sure! We live in the village just a bit down the river. Can you come? Can you? My friends will never believe me. Please come."

Suddenly Adahy became visible.

"Oh!" the girl gasped as she stumbled backward.

"Don't be afraid," he said softly. Then Awinita and Waya became visible as well.

"We won't hurt you," Awinita said.

"Four fairies!" the girl said with wonder. "Please come to my village," she invited them all. "Come and meet my people. We have always wanted to see fairies. We've heard the stories, but some of us don't believe them."

The fairies were also curious about the humans, so they agreed to follow the girl, but they insisted on staying invisible until they were sure that it would be safe. The girl happily agreed. They sent a quick thought to the deer, and the deer agreed to wait for them ... and happily graze while they waited.

They followed the gleeful girl along a path near the river. In the distance they could hear many voices talking and laughing. The fairies entered the village—which seemed huge to them—and saw the adult humans. They were giants! Waya, one of the tallest fairies in their village, didn't even come to their knees! The girl chattered continually ... to herself, or so it seemed to her people.

"Who are you talking to?" two women asked, confused.

"The fairies! I found fairies! At the river!"

The adults just rolled their eyes, "Come little one, there are no such things as fairies."

"Oh, but there are! Just like Grandfather's stories! And I can prove it!"

"Sure, sure," they smiled patronizingly. "Go see your mother."

The four fairies, still invisible, surveyed the village. The people wore what appeared to be animal skins, but without the fur. The women wore colorful beads around their necks and wrists, and their long black hair was braided down their backs. They were very active. It seemed that the giant people were busy getting ready for some kind of celebration. The wonderful smell of roasting nuts filled the air and some of the homes were decorated with greenery over the doors.

The fairies followed the girl to her home—a hut similar to their own homes, just much, much larger. The child tried to convince her mother that there were fairies in their hut, but her mother was busy and impatient with her daughter's wild tales. "No, I don't want to see your fairies. Why don't you go show them to your sister, and if she agrees, you can invite your invisible friends to the wedding."

Disappointed that her mother wouldn't even listen seriously to her, the little girl did just as her mother had suggested. Even though the child couldn't see the fairies, she faithfully said to the air, "Come on, fairies, let's go see my sister, the bride; she's getting married today. She'll be so glad to see you!"

Together they walked to a hut decorated with greenery and red berries over the doorway. "Leotie!" she called as she entered. "I have a surprise for you!"

"Hi, little one, I'm glad that you're here. I'm so bored. No one will let me do anything because it's my wedding day." The young woman was wearing a beautiful dress with intricate embroidery on the bodice, sleeves, and hem. Her long dark hair was neatly combed, and she had a wreath of fragrant gardenia flowers resting on top her head.

The little girl grinned, "I have a surprise for you. If I said that I had invited four fairies to your wedding, would you be happy? Would you like for them to be here?"

Leotie smiled at her silly little sister, "Sure I would, but as you know, they would be invisible and no one would be able to see them."

"No, not really," the child said mysteriously. "They're here ... now."

"OK," Leotie said, willing to go along with her sister's delusion. "Let's see them."

The child took Leotie by the hand and led her to a mat on the hut floor. "Now, don't be scared ... OK, fairies, please show Leotie that you're real."

Waya appeared.

Leotie gasped.

Waya disappeared.

"See!" the girl exclaimed gleefully. "They *are* real!"

Leotie's mouth hung open. She retrieved her wits and said incredulously, "I can't believe it! The stories *are* true!" Then she said to the place where Waya had appeared, "Please come back, I won't hurt you."

Then all the fairies appeared. Leotie's mouth hung open again, and then she smiled and said with genuine warmth, "Welcome!" Leotie studied the small fairies and was amazed at their beauty. They stood about one foot tall with dark hair much like her own. They had small pointed ears and their beautiful wings—which were folded behind their backs—were almost the same height as their bodies. They wore what looked to be woven grass held together with vines. "Where are you from?" she asked.

"We live west of here deep in the woods by a river. We're traveling to the east, to the great sea," Waya told the young woman.

"My name is Leotie, what are your names?" she politely asked.

"My name is Waya, this is Awinita, Adahy, and Dustu," he introduced them as he nodded to each in their group.

"Why are you traveling so far from home?" Leotie's little sister asked.

As Waya told of their journey, Leotie and her little sister kneeled in front of the fairies, listening intently. When he had finished their story, Leotie nodded in understanding. "We too have heard of the Savior who was foretold, but we didn't know He has now come! We need to tell my grandfather who is the Chief of our village," Leotie said, then hastily stood up.

"Wait, we really shouldn't be seen by your people!" Waya exclaimed as he flew up and touched her arm.

"Alright," Leotie paused, and then asked expectantly, "Will you follow me while invisible to see just my grandfather?"

"How far is your grandfather's hut?" Awinita asked.

"It's just across the village circle, just a few steps and we'll be there," Leotie answered happily.

"Can I come too?" Leotie's little sister asked.

"Of course, you're the one who found our new friends," Leotie smiled at her sister.

They all left Leotie's hut. With only herself and her sister visible, they all walked across the village, passing many neat huts. "Stay close," Leotie whispered behind her to the unseen fairies. After a short walk they arrived at the Chief's hut. "Grandfather, may I come in?"

A deep voice called from inside the hut, "Is that you, Leotie? Yes, come in." The fairies entered behind Leotie and her sister. Sitting on an animal skin was an impressive looking older man. He was large and muscular with only his hair—long and grey—revealing his true age.

Leotie and her sister sat down next to the chief. "Grandfather, we have something amazing to tell you ... uh, show you."

Laughing, the chief asked, "Are you having wedding jitters?"

"Oh no, it's not that. Do you remember the stories you would tell me when I was little? Stories about the little people of the forest?" Leotie asked.

"Of course I do. Those were your favorite. You would ask me to tell you the same story over and over again," the chief said, smiling at the pleasant memories.

"Well, Grandfather, we have a surprise for you!" Leotie's little sister chimed in excitedly.

Leotie turned around and seemingly talking to no one, she said, "You can show yourselves. It's safe."

The Chief looked puzzled at his granddaughters until suddenly four fairies appeared before him. "Ahhh!" he called out in shock as he fell backwards with surprise. He caught himself before falling all the way over, and then stared in disbelief at the small visitors.

"See, Grandfather? They're real! Fairies are real, just like you said," Leotie's sister exclaimed happily.

"Yes," the Chief breathed out in awe, "they certainly are!" As he stared at them, he was amazed that they looked very much like the people of his tribe, only much, much smaller—but with pointed ears and large beautiful wings. The one female had, what looked to be, a wing that had been badly burned. He wondered what had happened to her. Next to her was a boy, and behind them were two strong men—each with powerful looking wings. "So it's true! The stories passed down are real!" The Chief exclaimed in wonderment.

"Yes, Grandfather. And we just learned from our new friends that this is not the only legend that's true. The fairies have told us that the Messiah has been born in a faraway land and they're on a journey to find Him!" Leotie said in one breath.

"The Messiah has been born?" the Chief repeated while staring at the fairies.

"Yes, it's true," Waya was the first to speak. "He was born about thirty years ago. We received news of this from visitors who witnessed the Baby after His birth. We were told He would surely have started His ministry by now."

Waya, Adahy, Awinita, and Dustu continued to tell the Chief and his granddaughters all of what the visiting fairies had told them about their time with the Child Jesus. The Chief and his granddaughters listened intently until Awinita finally said, "Now we're on a journey across the great sea to find Him."

"This will be a very long and perilous journey, my new friends, but a worthy one. I will keep you in my thoughts and prayers," the Chief promised, smiling.

*

It was early afternoon and the fairies needed to leave. They apologized for not staying for Leotie's wedding, but the Chief and his granddaughters understood that they needed to be on their way. Leotie gathered extra food for them and then they all said their good-byes. The fairies promised to stop by their village when they returned and tell them all about their travels. The Chief and his granddaughters very much wanted to know more about the Savior, especially since He was a human, just like themselves.

Chapter 7

The Shore

The forest began to thin, and the deer were frightened to go farther out into the open. The fairies sent out thoughts in the animal spirit language, asking for any nearby eagles to come speak with them. When several came, they thanked the deer so very much for their help in bringing them so far, and then waved goodbye as they watched their animal friends disappear back into the forest.

One of the majestic eagles asked the fairies if they could fly themselves the several miles to the coast. Waya explained that they could indeed fly, but not for any great distance. They would have to stop and rest a number of times. (Out of kindness, he did not mention that one of their group had a crippled wing.) The eagles then graciously agreed to take them to the shore of the great sea. There were five eagles; one for each fairy and one to lead. Two of the eagles were the same two who the fairy visitors had asked to go and find the boat that they had used to cross the great sea. Those eagles had been flying high above, often watching for the fairies to arrive, and happy to finally see them.

One eagle touched his wing to the ground so that Awinita could easily climb up with her packs. Waya, Adahy, and Dustu flew up onto each of the other eagle's backs. The fairies tied their packs to themselves, hung onto the eagle's feathers, and nervously waited.

Dustu tightly clutched the eagle's head feathers. Chuckling, the eagle said to him, "Don't pull too hard on my feathers or I might end up being a bald eagle!"

Dustu giggled and eased his grip, "OK, sir, I won't."

Each great bird gently spread its wings and as carefully as possible, caught the wind and gracefully rose up into the air.

"Woo hoo!" Dustu yelled excitedly as they soared upward. "We can't fly this high! This is great!"

Waya, Adahy, and Awinita also delightfully laughed as the wind swept over them. The eagles chuckled as they flew higher and higher. "Hold on tight!" the lead eagle thought to them. "We won't go any higher, because the air gets rougher the higher we go."

Awinita twisted around to see Dustu. "You OK?" she called to him.

He grinned back. "This is so cool! Can we fly across the great sea?"

"No," his eagle interrupted and thought to him, "We can't fly that long without rest, and in the great sea, there is no place for us to land."

"Oh," Dustu thought back, disappointed, but then brightened. "That's OK; it's just so much fun."

Adahy called out to Awinita, "How about you? Are you doing OK?"

She laughed and called back to him, "Yes! I can't believe how wonderful this is! I wish we could fly like this all the time!"

Adahy laughed and Waya called out, "Me too!"

On and on they flew. The wind was cool, but the sun warmed their backs. They looked down at the tops of the trees as the eagles passed above them so quickly. It was glorious! As they flew onward, the air seemed to change. The familiar smell of pine and earth was replaced with a pleasant and refreshing saltiness. After what seemed to be a very short time, the lead eagle thought to them, "There's the shore!"

The fairies gasped at the distant sight. Water! Water from one side to the other—as far as their eyes could see! Endless water! They had finally arrived at the great sea.

The lead eagle turned a bit north and flew up the coastline. "Here it is!" he thought loudly. He flew over the shoreline and circled above. Right where some trees met the sandy beach rested the ark, hidden under the branches. All four fairies looked down from high above. "Wow!" exclaimed Dustu. "That's incredible!"

They all slowly descended to the shore. The lead eagle landed on the beach and the other eagles landed as gently as they could next to him. The fairies climbed down off their extraordinary friends. "We can't thank you enough for your help in getting us here," Waya said gratefully.

"Yes," the others thought as well, "thank you so very much."

The lead eagle swept his wing and slightly dipped his head, "You are very welcome." He then pointed with his beak and nodded toward some brush near the shore, "There's the boat. It's hidden there. I'll return tomorrow to help you find supplies. You'll need to ask the seagulls to find a whale to pull the boat for you. Now, we must go and hunt for some food." He raised his powerful wings and lifted off toward the sunset.

"Good journey," each of the four remaining eagles wished the fairies. Then, one by one, they raised their mighty wings and lifted up into the air. Soon they were all soaring out of sight.

The fairies marveled at the sand beneath their feet. They dug their toes into it ... it was so white and very fine—like the most finely ground seed flour. The beach extended as far as they could see in both directions—to the right and to the left—seemingly endless. In some places there was washed up debris—little pieces of wood and green slimy weeds. The sand was also littered by strange roundish things. Dustu picked one up—a shell of some kind. He admired its smooth surface, and then peered inside, trying to see if the creature that owned it was still there. No, it seemed empty, so he put it to his ear—just to be sure. He was surprised to hear the ocean inside! Of course there was no ocean in the shell, it just sounded like it.

Then the fairies turned to the sea. They were mesmerized by the awesome sight. The waves rolled and churned as they approached—then they crashed and rushed toward the shore— overlapping each other. Dustu crept to the changing line of wet sand. He carefully stepped onto it—it was very cool under his feet. Then a foamy wave rushed toward him, thinning as it approached. Dustu let it wash coldly across his feet. Suddenly he felt the sand under his feet being pulled away, and he nearly lost his balance. He jumped back as Awinita warned, "Be careful!"

It was getting late; the sun was down below the tree tops in the distance. Waya said, "Let's camp here. Tomorrow we'll check out the boat." He looked over at the dark and gloomy brush where the ark was well hidden. "I hope it's in good condition, or our journey will be over before it begins."

*

Dustu was the first to rise the next morning ... he had to go "relieve" himself. He wiped the sleep out of his eyes and walked a bit away from the camp. He stood facing a tree with his back to the beach. He suddenly realized that he wasn't alone. Several strange birds were watching him intently.

"Hey, can a guy get some privacy?" he thought at them.

Ignoring his comment, a bird shrilled back, "Who are you?"

"No, *what* are you!" another bird squawked.

"Yeah, *what* are you? Never saw anything like *you* before."

Dustu turned and thought to them, "I'm a fairy, of the inland fairy people."

"What's a fairy?" another bird said in a squeaky voice.

Then another bird asked, "Got any food?"

Several more seagulls flew over and joined them. "Yeah, got any food?"

"Go away!" The seagulls squawked. "We saw him first!"

"You have food, don't you? I want some!"

"Go away!"

"Try and make me, jerk!" The silly birds began squawking with each other. "You're not the boss of me!"

"I don't make jerks!"

"I know you're a jerk, but what am I?"

"I know you are, but what am I?"

"You're stupid!"

"Am not!"

"Are too!"

"Am not!"

"Are too!"

"You have a little beak!"

"Do not!"

"Do too!"

"Well, you're ugly!"

"No, you're ugly and you *stink*!"

"Do not!"

"Do too!"

"SHUT UP!" Dustu shrieked, holding his fists over his ears. "You're making me crazy!"

There was momentarily a stunned silence. Then Waya, who had silently walked up behind them all, asked, "What's going on here?"

"Do you have food?" the birds turned to Waya.

"Give us food!"

"Hold on, now." Waya said with a calm voice. "We don't have any food that you would be interested in, I'm sure. Don't you eat fish? We finished our fish a day ago."

"We eat anything ... what *do* you have?" the birds asked eagerly, coming closer.

Suddenly the mighty eagle from the night before swooped down. "Back off, idiots," he thought loudly at the seagulls. "You are quite capable of fishing for yourselves instead of begging."

Suddenly the gulls were amazingly silent.

"But, I have an idea," the eagle thought to them. "I will catch some fish for you right now, if you agree to help the fairies find a whale who will be willing to pull a boat across the great sea. Deal?"

"Yes, sir," the seagulls thought back respectfully.

"OK then, I'll be right back," the eagle thought to them, and then he took flight and was gone.

Within minutes the eagle was back. He opened his talons and dropped some fish among the gulls, which they greedily attacked. "Mine!" they each squawked shrilly. "Mine!"

After a few more minutes he was back with another load, and again dropped them to the greedy birds. After four loads, he soared up into the sky again and brought a fifth load—which he gave to the fairies. "You need to replenish your supplies before starting on your sea voyage," he thought to them.

The fairies were eager to inspect the ark, but they realized that the eagle was right—they needed supplies later but also needed some right now. They thanked the eagle, and he suggested that he fly them to a nearby wooded area so they could hunt for seeds, nuts, and greens. The fairies thanked the eagle for his offer.

"I'll go," Waya volunteered.

"I want to go too!" Dustu exclaimed.

"Sir," Waya asked the kind eagle, "Can you carry both of us?"

The eagle chuckled, "Let's find out!" So, Waya and Dustu flew up and together sat on his back. The eagle spread his powerful wings and rose up into the air.

Adahy and Awinita stayed behind. They gathered wood, then cleaned and smoked the fish. Meanwhile, the well-fed seagulls sat nearby on the warm sand with their eyes closed, sleeping.

After a few hours, the eagle returned, but without Waya and Dustu. Instead he had a large coarsely woven grass pouch hanging from his talons which was filled with greens, herbs, and berries. He dropped it near the fairy's camp and took off back toward the woods again. Later, he returned with Dustu who had a full pack tied to his back. Then he went to retrieve Waya with his full pack.

The fairies thanked the generous eagle, and he said that he would be back to see if they needed anything else—and to assure that the seagulls had fulfilled their end of the bargain. As he thought that, he turned to stare sternly at the gulls. Then he was gone.

The day was spent, but the fairies were very grateful to the eagle. They had planned to hunt for more supplies when they got near the shore, because the trip across the sea would take several months. Thanks to the eagle, they would be able to start their journey sooner.

Chapter 8

The Ark

The next morning, after eating a breakfast of nuts and berries, they began to uncover the ark. They removed the brush, and more brush ... and even more brush. It took all morning, but when it was fully uncovered, they couldn't believe how big it was. They all stood next to the boat and marveled at the construction. It was huge! The base was like a big rectangle. It seemed to be the length of 23 full-grown bucks, and the width of about 4 big bucks. And it was tall—about twice as tall as a human man. Waya remembered that the visiting fairies had explained that this boat was one quarter the size of Noah's original ark but made in the same proportions, so it would also float stably in the rough sea waters.

Waya and Adahy fluttered their wings and flew up to the top of the boat. They landed onto the long wooden deck. In the center of that deck and running down the length of it was a long rectangular structure. It had windows all along the sides of it, but they were tightly shut—locked from the inside. They walked around the structure until they came to a door, which after lifting the latch, opened for them. Inside was a long room with a wood floor. It was very dark and the air smelled stale. With what little light the open door gave them, they entered. They let their eyes adjust to the darkness, and then began to unlatch and prop open each window they came to. Soon they were all open, allowing the fresh salty air and the sunshine to flood in.

Suddenly the boy's voice from the doorway exclaimed, "Whoa! This is so cool! May I come in?"

"Sure," Waya said to Dustu. "Come on in."

"Wow!" Dustu said in awe as he looked all around and then up at the peaked roof above.

In the center of the long room was a stone fire-pit. Above it was a type of "door" in the roof, and after closer examination, they found that it cleverly opened and closed by ropes and a pulley.

Awinita walked in the sand along the outside of the ark— looking for any damage to the wooden hull from its initial voyage. She ran her hand along the side, admiring the perfect craftsmanship. Could this boat again successfully cross the dangerous great sea? She came to the bow of the ark and noticed thick long straps coming out of the front. The extra lengths of the straps were piled high in front of the boat. She thought to herself, *these must be the straps that the whale will pull us with*. She bent down and tried to lift one, but it was too heavy for her delicate arms. She thought to herself *how are we going to get this into the water, when even the straps to pull the ark are so heavy?* Suddenly she felt a rush of air as the eagle landed beside her.

"Wondering how to get the ark into the water?" the eagle asked. Awinita nodded. "Don't worry. When the tide comes in, this boat will have some water around it—not enough for it to float away, but enough to make hauling it out easier. The local bucks can help pull the straps out a bit into the water. Then the dolphins can pull them to the whale, and he will be strong enough to tug it out of the sand. I'll find the bucks when you're ready—I know their favorite grazing spot."

"What are 'dolphins'?" Awinita asked, curiously.

The eagle laughed, "Oh, you'll love them! They are the most playful and curious creatures of the sea. You'll be quite entertained by their antics."

Awinita looked up at the boat's high bow. Noticing her looking above, the eagle asked, "Have you seen the inside?"

"No, not yet," she answered.

"Do you need a lift up to the deck?" the kind eagle offered.

"Yes, please, if you don't mind."

The eagle lowered his wing for her to climb up onto his back. "Hold tight!"

In a few seconds they were up and on the deck. "Thank you," she said as she slid down off his wing.

"Hey, Awinita, come check out this room!" Dustu called from inside the ark.

As she stepped through the open door she was awestruck. The wide room was very long. She walked along one of the sides and saw shelves and storage bins that were secured to the wall. She nodded in approval as they would need proper places to put their provisions for the long voyage. She walked farther down and noticed hammocks hanging from the ceiling.

Dustu ran ahead of her and jumped into one of the hammocks. "This one's mine!" he shouted out. But, instead of him lying secure in the hammock, he had jumped into it so hard that it swung up and flipped over, dumping him—plop—onto the deck!

As he lay stunned on his back, Awinita rushed to him and anxiously asked, "Are you hurt?"

"No," Dustu answered ruefully as he stood up. "I don't think so."

"Can you at least *try* to be more careful?" Awinita scolded, shaking her head as she dusted off his backside.

Just then Adahy walked up to them. "What's going on?"

Dustu glanced up at Awinita with a pleading look. She turned to Adahy and answered, "Nothing much ... what's at the other end of this room?"

"There's another door, but it's stuck. I'm going to get Waya to help me open it."

They could hear footsteps on the roof. "That's Waya! I'll get him!" Dustu exclaimed, trying to be helpful. As he rushed off, he said quickly to Awinita, "I'll be careful."

"So, what do you think?" Adahy asked.

"I think this boat is remarkable," she answered.

"Yes, I think so too. The hull seems sound. The inside in here is absolutely huge, so we'll have plenty of storage area for supplies. There's a fire-pit for cooking, and there are even hammocks all ready for us. All we need are supplies and we'll be ready to go."

"Yes," she smiled up to Adahy. She paused and then asked quietly, "Do you think we'll make it?"

Adahy was surprised. "Yes, I do. Why ... don't you?"

She shrugged. "It's such a long journey. What if we run out of supplies? What if we get in a storm and this boat sinks? What if we ...?"

Adahy touched his fingers gently to her lips and reassured softly, "Don't worry. I thought about this on the way here. I had my doubts too, but then I realized that Angels had told the fairies to go and tell all the fairy world of Jesus. They had done that, and then they came to our land from across the great sea—safely in this boat, I might add—to continue the Angels' request. So, I figure the Great Creator protected them, and He'll protect us as well."

Awinita smiled up at him, "You do know how to make a girl feel better, don't you?"

"I try, but especially for you," he smiled.

Awinita felt her cheeks turn red.

Then Dustu and Waya entered the room. "The roof looks nice and tight. It shouldn't leak," Waya announced.

"Great," Adahy nodded, and then pointed to the other end of the great room. "Can you come help me get that door open?"

*

During the rest of the afternoon, Awinita disconnected the hammocks and then she and Dustu went out to the edge of the deck and shook the dust off them. Then she proceeded to clean out the bins and wipe down the shelves. While she was busy cleaning, Dustu went to check out a curious portion of the deck that had a rail around it, but was raised up a bit and jutted out of the stern (the rear) of the ark. Adahy and Waya were busy bringing in the supplies that they had accumulated so far, but Dustu called for Waya to come over to him.

"Waya, what's this for? This sticks out over the water and has a hole in it. Is it for a fishing line?"

Waya looked carefully at it and then he grinned, "No, it's not for fishing ... it's for pooping."

"What?" Dustu exclaimed, "For pooping?"

"Yes, Dustu, it's for us to use on the long voyage ... we have to 'go' somewhere, right?"

"Uh, yeah," Dustu replied warily. "But it's so ... out in the open."

"Don't worry, son, no one will watch," he said smiling as he ruffled the boy's hair.

*

Dustu explored a bit more inside and found a pull-up door in the floor. Waya and Adahy raised it up and found that the space below was totally dark, so they had to wait for evening when the fireflies came out to give them some "light" help.

As evening approached, Waya found and asked a large group of fireflies to come and fly down into the darkness within the belly of the boat. Waya and Adahy carefully flew down the narrow staircase and into the depth. Dustu watched eagerly from the top step as they descended down into the gloom. "What's down there?" he called out.

With a soft flickering glow, the fireflies illuminated the darkness below. After a few moments, Waya shouted up, "There's nothing down here—just the bottom of the boat." Both he and Adahy flew up the stairs, and then the fireflies swarmed up and out of the darkness as well. Waya thanked the little insects, and off they flew.

"I'm glad there's nothing down there that we need to be concerned with—because it stinks a bit."

*

Within the next few days, with the eagle's help, they gathered more supplies. The seagulls fulfilled their promise and found a whale who agreed to help pull the ark. Along with the whale came several curious dolphins.

"We found a whale for you!" one of the seagulls squawked loudly to the eagle.

"Just like we promised!" another joined in.

"And, we brought some dolphins too, so maybe we can get more fish as a reward?"

"Yes, yes, yes, Mr. Eagle, more fish. Please?"

"Why didn't you just get some for yourself when you were out there?" the eagle sensibly asked.

They looked at each other, confused, and then one said, "We didn't think of it."

The eagle rolled his eyes and said, "OK, I'll be right back." He spread his large wings out and off he flew. The seagulls eagerly danced around on the sand as they waited for their reward.

Chapter 9

Into the Sea

The eagle called the three dolphins to come closer to shore so that Waya, Adahy, and Dustu could fly the short distance to them. Then the eagle made the introductions. The three dolphins were named Tinka, Binka, and Finn; they were brother and sisters. The dolphins and the fairies had never seen or heard of each other before, so they were both curious. Waya thanked the dolphins for volunteering to help, and the dolphins bobbed their gray heads up and down in response. Then the eagle suggested that the fairies go to speak with the nice whale who would be helping them. The whale was in deeper water quite a bit farther off from the coastline, so the eagle asked if the dolphins would be so kind to give the fairies a lift.

They graciously agreed.

Waya, Adahy, and Dustu each flew down to the waiting dolphins and landed gently on the back of their heads. The dolphins were smooth and wet with seawater, but the fairies were able to hang on. Then the dolphins swam very carefully out toward the giant whale. Waya and Adahy cheerfully thought-chatted with their dolphins, Tinka and Binka, as did Dustu with Finn, but Dustu was very curious about the breathing "hole" in the top of Finn's head. He leaned forward a bit and tried to peek down into it. He wondered if he would be able to see the dolphin's brain, but all he saw was darkness. Dustu glanced up to see Waya's eyes wide as he shook his head "No!" Then Waya silently mouthed, "Don't be rude!" Embarrassed, Dustu leaned back and continued to thought-talk with Finn. Even though the dolphins were swimming slowly and carefully, they reached the whale quickly.

Awinita watched from the shore. As the dolphins carried the fairies, the eagle flew back to shore and landed next to her. "Come, you can go too." The eagle lowered his wing for Awinita, and she climbed up and sat on his back. He gracefully soared up and flew out to sea. The great whale was patiently waiting for them. Not seeing them, just before the eagle was to land on him the whale blew a great plume of air and water up high into the sky.

"Whoa!" The eagle banked sharply to the side, avoiding most of the force of the spray.

"Oops! Sorry," the whale apologized. "I didn't realize that you were so close."

"No harm done," the eagle laughed. "I guess a little shower won't hurt me. Are you OK, Awinita?"

Awinita shook her wings and wiped the dripping water off her face. "I'm fine. The water is ... very refreshing."

They landed on the great whale's back, and Awinita slid down and off the eagle's wing. Shortly after, the dolphins and their riders arrived. Waya, Adahy, and Dustu flew up off the dolphins, thanking them for the ride, and joined Awinita and the eagle on the whale.

The eagle introduced them to Marco, the whale. Marco knew about the ark, because he had helped pull it for the other fairies. He graciously agreed to help again in this new quest. Waya formally thanked him as did the other fairies.

Just then, the three dolphins shot up out of the ocean water and spun around in mid-air! Then they dove down into the depths. "Show-offs!" Marco called to them.

Their heads broke the surface of the water and they giggled, "How about that?"

"Wow!" Dustu shouted. "That was great! Do it again!"

Marco laughed and said, "Children will be children."

Again, the dolphins shot up out of the water and did a flip, and then disappeared into the waves. "Can I ride you while you do that?" Dustu eagerly asked when the dolphins surfaced again.

Before the dolphins could answer, Waya exclaimed, "NO! Absolutely not. Dustu, fairies cannot swim ... or did you forget that?"

"Oh ... right," Dustu frowned.

"You can't swim?" Finn asked incredulously. "We've never met anyone who couldn't swim!"

"What about me?" the eagle interrupted.

"Oh, yeah, that's right. I never thought of that!" Finn laughed.

*

After a short visit, the group returned to the shore. The seagulls were picking at something on the sand. Dustu went to investigate—it was a dead monster that had washed up onto the shore!

"What is *that* thing?" he asked the busily feeding birds.

"It's ours! You can't have any!" they squawked at him, and continued pulling it apart and greedily eating it.

"Don't worry! I don't want any of *that*. What is it, anyway?" Dustu asked, peering closer to the strange creature that had many arms ... or feet, depending on how you look at it.

"It's an octopus, now go away!" they demanded.

"No problem ... yuk."

*

After a couple more days of gathering supplies, smoking fish, and filling the water barrels which they had found on the ark, they were ready. The eagle flew to the favorite grazing spot of the deer, and asked two bucks to come and help—which they generously agreed to do. When the bucks arrived, the fairies explained what they needed to accomplish. There were two long straps attached to the front of the boat, which were also securely tied together at the very end—probably so that the whale could get a good mouth grip on them.

The bucks understood what they needed to do. They bent their heads down and twisted the straps into their antlers. With a firm grip, they pulled the straps out straight along the shoreline, assuring that there were no tangles. Then they walked the straps back along the shore and into the surf. With the waves washing higher and higher across their muscular chests, the bucks walked the long straps out into the water as far as they could. The waves weren't too high, so they managed to get them out a good bit. They then lowered their heads and shook the straps out of their antlers, letting them sink into the water.

Later, when the tide was at its highest, Finn dove down and got the end of the joined straps into his mouth. Then Tinka and Binka put their mouths on the side of each strap, and the three of them lifted the straps off the sandy bottom and swam them out to Marco. Because the tide was high, Marco was able to get—cautiously—rather close to the shoreline.

The fairies stood on a sand dune, away from the ark, and waited. The high tide water swirled around the base of the entire boat as the waves swept in and out. Suddenly, the straps lifted off the sandy beach and became taunt. Then the ark began to slide forward! As they watched with fascination, the big boat gradually slid across the sand and into the surf. In just a few seconds, it was floating!

"All aboard!" Waya called out, laughing. "Let's go!"

Grinning, Dustu flew to the gently moving ark. Waya and Adahy each took Awinita's arms, lifted her, and flew to their waiting boat as well. The eagle landed on the roof of the ark's center structure. "I'll go tell Marco that you're ready to go, right?"

Waya flew up to the roof and stood in front of the eagle. "Yes, we're ready … we don't know how to thank you for all your help," he began.

The eagle cut him off, "No thanks needed. Just come back safely and tell me everything you learned about the Savior. He is also *our* Lord, you know, so your journey will benefit us all."

Then he spread his great wings and soared up into the sky. He circled the ark once as the fairies waved and shouted, "Good-bye and thank you!" Then he headed toward where Marco waited.

Chapter 10

On Our Way

The ark started moving forward out to sea. As they were towed further out, the fairies watched the shore shrink smaller and smaller until it completely disappeared from their sight. Now, all they could see was water … water stretched out in all directions … water everywhere.

Tinka, Binka, and Finn raced ahead of the bow. Dustu jumped up a bit and leaned over the chest high railing and thought-called to his new friends, "How fast can you swim?"

"Fast!" Finn called back as he leapt over a wave.

"Woo hoo!" all the dolphins laughed with glee as they glided through the water. The fairies watched the playful dolphins as they giggled and jumped along in front of the ark.

Awinita stood at the railing and closed her eyes as the sun warmed her face. It felt so strange with the salty air blowing across her wings and the movement of the boat below her feet. She was surprised how peaceful it all felt. Suddenly, Marco blew out a burst of air and water that sent a cool mist across her face. She smiled and thought, *this will be a successful journey.*

*

The first day of their voyage turned to night. The ark moved gently with the ocean waves, but no one became sea-sick. In fact, it gently rocked the fairies to sleep in their hammocks. They all slept soundly—and snored loudly. All except for Awinita; she had the same nightmare that tormented her sleep so often—the great fire—and she woke in a sweat. She couldn't get back to sleep, so she quietly rolled out of her hammock and tip-toed to the door of the long room and stepped out onto the deck. The others continued to snore behind her.

A cool breeze blew her hair as she walked over to the side of the boat and leaned against the railing. The night sky was brilliant with millions of sparkling white stars above. It was almost magical! There was one star that was brighter than all the others. She stared at it in wonder when a deep voice from behind startled her and made her jump.

"Can't sleep, huh?" the voice said.

"Adahy, you nearly scared the life out of me!"

"Sorry," he grinned. "I saw you when you opened the door to come out here."

"I tried to be quiet; I didn't mean to wake anyone," Awinita apologized.

"No, you didn't. Who can sleep with Waya and Dustu snoring like frogs?"

"I was sure *you* were one of them making all that noise," she accused him, smiling.

"No, not me!" he laughed. Then he looked down and saw that she had the rose quartz in her hand. "It's not working, is it?" he asked sadly.

She looked up at him and saw him nod to her hand. She shrugged and said, "Maybe not, but I still like it very much." She turned back to the railing, "Do you see that bright star over there? I wonder if it's like the star that those men saw and followed to find the infant Savior."

Adahy leaned his arm across the rail and studied the brilliant star. "Maybe ... but probably not, because that star doesn't move, and theirs did—because they *followed* it."

"Yes, you're right. They *did* follow it," she mused. "That star up there is so pretty; I can only imagine how beautiful the star that led them was."

Their conversation was suddenly interrupted. "You two should be sleeping," Marco thought loudly to them.

"Oh, hi Marco," Adahy thought back. "We didn't realize you were right here."

"I had to take a break from pulling. There was a large group of krill going by and I couldn't pass that up. Yum."

Awinita and Adahy laughed with him. "Please, take a break whenever you wish to. We don't want to work you too hard."

"Me? Work too hard? I'm as strong as a whale ... wait a minute ... I *am* a whale!" Marco joked. "Seriously, though, why are you two up at this late hour?"

"I had a nightmare," Awinita sighed. "Again."

"I understand completely," Marco said with compassion. "I sometimes get them too. When I was but a young calf, I was attacked by sharks. My mother fought them off, but they injured her. Some of them you can reason with, but most of them are just eating machines, and don't care who they hurt."

"Oh, Marco, I'm so sorry to hear that. Did your mother recover?"

"Yes," Marco sighed, "eventually she did—mostly. So now when I wake from those nightmares, I just try to focus on happy memories—like my first delicious taste of krill. But sometimes that doesn't even work."

"Yes," Awinita nodded. "I know what you mean."

Not wanting to bring up more painful memories from their friend, Adahy and Awinita bid Marco "good night" and went back inside to try to get some sleep.

*

The next morning was sunny and bright. The dolphins were playing chase with the ark as Marco pulled it swiftly through the gentle waves. "Hey, Dustu, want some green stuff?" Finn called up to the boy.

"What do you mean 'green stuff'?" Dustu called back.

"You know, green stuff, the things that grow in the ocean. Humans eat it, so you probably can too," Finn assured him.

Awinita joined them and thought to them, "Yes, thank you, I would like to try it."

Finn disappeared beneath the waves, with giggling Tinka and Binka close behind. Waya and Adahy joined Awinita and Dustu, and waited with them for their sea friends. Soon, three dolphin heads popped up. They each had a long strand of a green plant hanging out of their mouths.

"Hold on!" Adahy called to them as he unrolled a rope that was tied to the deck railing. It splashed down into the water and he climbed down it. Holding onto the rope, he leaned over to take a seaweed strand from Tinka's mouth. First carefully tucking his wings close to his back, he threw it over his shoulder. Next he took one from Binka's mouth and then a really long one from Finn, and tossed them over his shoulder as well. He thanked the dolphins and then climbed back up the rope.

Waya helped him back over the rail and Awinita took the seaweed from him. She looked at it and sniffed it, then bravely took a tiny taste of it. "Humm, not bad ... tastes a bit salty," she murmured. "We can eat this and use it to season the fish we have." She leaned over the rail and thought-called to the dolphins, "Thank you!"

The dolphins chirped back, "Anytime!" And then they disappeared under the water.

"Let me try some," Dustu said as he stepped forward and tore off a large leaf. He stuffed it into his mouth and started to chew. His eyes grew wide and his face grimaced. He bent over and violently spit it out. "Eeeyuk!" he gagged. "That's just nasty!" Then he dry-heaved.

Waya and Adahy laughed loudly, and even Awinita had trouble not smiling at Dustu's misery. "You tried to eat too much!" she said, hiding her giggle.

"Paah! Paah!" Dustu spit. Then he pawed madly at his tongue, trying to rid his mouth of any trace of the seaweed. "Gaaaa! I think they tried to poison me!" Then he gagged again.

Awinita's face strained as she tried not to laugh at Dustu's antics. But it was too much. She laughed out loud—she really tried not to, but she just couldn't help it.

Chapter 11

Ocean Lights

The days passed uneventfully. The dolphins sometimes brought the fairies fresh fish, and occasionally more seaweed. Then one night, just before they were going to go inside and go to sleep, they saw a strange sight. In the distance there was something glowing in the moonlight—something *big*!

Waya thought-called to the dolphins and Marco, "Do you see that up ahead? The water is glowing bright blue!"

"Yes," Marco thought back, "I've seen this many times. It's caused by a great mass of tiny little algae. When they are disturbed, they make that brilliant blue color."

"Oh, they're so beautiful!" Awinita smiled in awe, watching the moonlight reflect off the glowing algae.

Just then, three dolphin heads broke the water's surface. "Watch this!" they laughed and then dove back down. A few seconds later they had reached the blue place and began jumping and thrashing about. Suddenly the water sparkled and glowed even more brilliantly as it splashed all around the playful dolphins. The sight was magical!

Marco chuckled, changed direction, and pulled the ark toward the bright blue water. In no time at all, the boat was surrounded by glowing blue water droplets that seemed to twinkling as they splashed up.

"Wow!" Dustu exclaimed. "That is just too cool!"

"I've never seen anything so beautiful in all my life!" Awinita marveled.

"Amazing!" Waya agreed.

"Awesome," Adahy grinned.

"Finn!" Dustu called. "Would you let me sit on you so I can touch the sparkling water?"

"Sure!" Finn called back, "Come on down!"

Dustu fluttered his wings and rose up over the railing and down onto Finn's head. Finn stayed still while Dustu dipped his hand into the water and swished it about. The water glittered a more dazzling blue at his touch. He lifted his hand and the glowing drops fell from his fingers tips back into the sea. He played with the amazing water until their boat cleared the brilliant blue patch. Marco then changed his direction to get the ark back on course.

The next morning was clear and bright, and the fairies went through their usual routines. The washed their faces, ate breakfast, cleaned up, and then waited for lunch. The trip wasn't very exciting. Sometimes, when the sea was calm enough, Dustu rode on Finn's head as he swam, circling around and around the ark. Awinita kept going over their stocks of supplies, Adahy studied the construction of the ark, and Waya often flew over to Marco and rode on his back while they talked together.

Chapter 12

Sharks!

One day, Awinita and Adahy were sitting on the deck together, enjoying the sunshine. Dustu and Waya were on the roof, looking out over the unending water all around, when they all heard a scream of pain.

"What was that!" Waya shouted as he flew down to the deck.

The fairies ran to the railing and looked down. The water below splashed about violently. Another scream of terror shocked their minds. "It's Tinka!" Dustu yelled.

A great dark shape swept by their boat. "Marco!" Waya shouted out his thought. "What's happening?"

"Sharks!" Marco quickly thought back, as he dove into the depths.

The fairies waited breathlessly. Then Tinka's head broke the surface and she gasped for a breath. She cried out, "They hurt me! They wanted to eat me!"

"Are you alright?" Awinita anxiously called down to her.

"Noooo, it hurts! It h … hurts!" she continued to cry. Then she almost rolled onto her side.

Finn and Binka broke the surface. "No!" they shouted together, "Tinka! Don't roll over!"

"It hurts so much," Tinka moaned.

"Maybe I can help her!" Awinita thought anxiously as she ran over to the rope that was still attached to the rail.

"Wait!" Adahy called out after her. He flew to the rope. "Let me help you!"

Finn frantically called up to them, "How can you help her?"

Dustu leapt up and hung half way over the rail top and hollered down to the dolphins, "Girl fairies have the gift of healing!"

A look of hope crossed Tinka's eyes, as she continued to moan in agony.

Adahy uncoiled the rope and let it drop into the sea. Then he flew over the rail and grabbed the rope. He held his hand out to Awinita. She took it and quickly climbed over. He slid down a bit as she clung onto the rope just above him. Then they both slid down carefully. Adahy stayed close below and next to her, in case she lost her grip. They reached the water and felt it splash up onto them. Awinita slid down so that she was even with Adahy, then she reached down toward the water, reaching for Tinka. Finn and Binka gently nosed Tinka toward the boat side, close enough for Awinita to touch her. There was an awful wound on Tinka's side— a bleeding gash in her flesh.

As Awinita touched Tinka, she felt the warm healing gift flow from her hands. Tinka shuddered as the healing entered her body. She closed her eyes and moaned again, but this time with relief. "Oh, that's wonderful," she gasped. "Thank you, thank you, thank you."

Finn and Binka watched with amazement. "This is truly a wonderful gift you have!"

In intense concentration, Awinita did not speak, but continued to touch Tinka for many minutes. Adahy held her as well as the rope. He could feel her weakening. "Are you OK?" he whispered into her ear. She didn't answer, but continued to touch Tinka. Adahy could see tiny beads of water appearing on her skin. It wasn't seawater—it was sweat from her exertion. Suddenly Awinita almost lost her grip on the rope. Adahy quickly caught her as she became limp. "That's enough for now," he said emphatically. He lifted her up and repositioned her in his arms and fluttered his powerful wings. He let go of the rope and flew up with Awinita, who was now fully unconscious in his arms. He laid her carefully on the deck. Waya and Dustu rushed to her side.

"Is she OK?" Tinka called out anxiously from below. "Is she OK?"

Waya answered, "She will be. She just needs to recover a bit. Don't worry."

"Oh, I hope so!" Tinka replied, relieved. "She's wonderful. I feel so much better now."

"Wow!" Finn said in amazement. "Your wound isn't bleeding anymore, and it doesn't look so ... well, like it did."

"I can't believe it," Binka agreed. "This is amazing!"

Just then the huge shape of Marco broke the water's surface. "I just had a talk with the sharks. I explained about our journey, and they understand. They promised to feed elsewhere and to tell others of their kind to leave us alone. They too want to know about the Savior of the world.

"Do you trust them?" Waya asked.

Marco thought for a moment and then answered, "Not entirely. Eating is their reason for living, so we still need to be alert and aware of them."

Awinita began to stir, so Adahy lifted her head and shoulders to lean against his chest. "Are you OK?" he asked gently, still concerned.

She nodded, and took a deep breath. "I've never had that happen to me before," she whispered.

"I'll go make you some rosehip tea!" Dustu volunteered.

"That will help, thank you," Awinita said weakly, smiling at her brother.

"And put some of the rose honey in it!" Adahy called to him.

"OK!" Dustu shouted over his shoulder.

As Dustu rushed off, Adahy helped Awinita to sit up. Then Waya knelt next to her and said softly, "You had us worried."

"I'll be fine after I rest a bit," she assured him.

The dolphins called to the fairies, "Is she OK now?"

Adahy and Waya helped her to her feet, and held her arms as she slowly walked to the railing. "I'm OK," she thought to them. "I just need to rest some."

"I don't know how to thank you," Tinka thought gratefully to her.

"You don't have to, friends help each other, just like you are helping us."

"You have given Tinka such a marvelous gift," Binka added.

"No, it's not *my* gift, it's a gift given to our kind from the Great Creator—it's His gift, not mine, to be used to help others."

Chapter 13

Are We There Yet?

The long trip across the great sea was becoming more and more tiresome. Tinka's wound was now mostly healed, with only a scar to remind her to always be watchful.

"Are we there yet?" Dustu often asked.

And Marco's answer was always, "Not yet, but soon."

Dustu complained of the boredom, but in truth, the rest of the fairies were just as bored. There was only so much they could do to occupy the long hours. Waya told stories he had heard from his youth. Adahy talked of hunting and fishing. Awinita repeated the healing stories the medicine woman had told her. Dustu made up "fairy" stories—he had a great imagination.

Then one day, the dolphins brought a new dolphin friend—Chipper—to visit them. Chipper was full of information. He was from the area not far from land—the land they were headed for! He and Marco conversed, and it was confirmed that their journey would soon come to an end. Chipper swam with them and when Marco left briefly to feed, he told them a story.

"I know you are on a quest to find Jesus. Well, my Mom heard from a seabird who heard from a hawk who heard from a big lady fish in the Sea of Galilee who said that she saw Jesus walk on top of the water!"

"Really?" Dustu asked in astonishment.

"Yes," Chipper nodded his grey head up and down eagerly. "She said that there was a storm coming and a boat with the friends of Jesus was being tossed about. It was late at night—just before dawn—when she saw a figure of a human *walking* across the sea toward the boat. She could hardly believe what she was seeing! Two people on the boat also saw him and were afraid. They didn't know who—or *what* it was. They thought maybe it was a ghost or something! Then Jesus called out to them and told them that it was He and for them not to be afraid. They were still spooked, and the big guy—the one they call Peter—called out to Jesus asking Him to let him come out on the water and walk on it too! So Jesus said, 'OK,' and Peter got out of the boat and walked on water just like Jesus was doing!"

Dustu looked at the dolphin with doubt and asked, "Are you sure? That's just unbelievable."

Chipper stared into Dustu's eyes and said solemnly, "Yes, it's totally true. Dolphins do NOT lie. Ever!"

Then a seagull landed on the roof of the ark. "That's for sure," he thought with a squawk. "No one can bribe them to not tell on you, either. I pooped all over some sheep on a human's boat, and I offered a fish to a dolphin who saw it all—for him not to tell— but he refused it and told the sheep that I was the guilty one."

Dustu giggled.

"Well, you'd better not poop on *our* boat!" Adahy warned the seagull.

"OK, OK," the seagull assured him. "Don't get upset, I'll control myself."

Then a little yellow bird landed on the dolphin's head. "Do you mind if I sit here for a moment?" he chirped.

"No, I don't mind ... just stay still, because your feet tickle." Then Chipper continued with his story, "While Peter was on the water with Jesus, the storm kicked up, and the wind howled and the waves got rougher. Peter was afraid and began to sink! He called out to Jesus to save him, so Jesus reached out His hand and pulled Peter back up. Then Jesus asked him why he had such little faith and why did he doubt Him. Then all the men on that boat worshiped Jesus and said that it was true that He was the Son of God."

"Wow," the fairies said together.

"Well, I can top that!" the little bird chirped excitedly. "When I was a chick, I landed on a window sill of a human house. It was very sad because the little girl who lived there had just died. Friends and relatives were at the house and were trying to comfort the parents. The little girl's mother was crying so very hard and loud—that's why I was there. I heard her crying and I was curious about what had happened.

"When Jesus came to the house of the grieving family, He told the crowd outside that the little girl wasn't dead—she was just sleeping. All the people laughed at Him and some even called Him bad names ... I won't repeat them here ... but trust me, they were *very* insulting. When He went inside the house, He only let His friends Peter, James, and John come in with Him. He went into the little girl's room with the parents and knelt by her bed. He took her hand and said, 'Young lady, rise!' And guess what? I saw the little girl's spirit enter back into her! Then I saw her chest rise up as she took a deep breath. I jumped back and nearly fell out of the window! She was alive! Then He pulled her up and she stood!

"I saw this with my own two eyes, and it's still hard to believe! Even the little girl's parents were shocked, but then the mother threw her arms around her daughter and cried even louder, but now her tears were of joy. Her amazed father had tears running down into his beard. He knelt before Jesus, thanking and thanking Him, but Jesus just said for them to give the girl food. Then He told the parents not to tell what had happened. But it was too late, because the people outside realized that the girl had been raised from the dead, and they told everyone of the miracle made by Jesus, the Nazarene.

The fairies were amazed. Even the animals knew of Jesus and were telling everyone of His incredible miracles. "Wow," Waya said wistfully, "I can hardly wait to meet Him."

Chapter 14

The Storm

Waya and Adahy stood on the roof of the ark, looking at the gathering dark clouds. "Looks like a storm coming," Waya said grimly.

"It sure looks like it," Adahy agreed. "And it seems to be coming fast."

"We need to tighten everything down," Waya nodded.

Dustu and Awinita walked out onto the deck and looked up at them as they flew down from the roof. "What were you doing up there?" Dustu asked.

"Storm coming," Adahy pointed toward the angry looking clouds in the distance.

"And it's coming fast," Waya added. "Dustu, help me close up the windows."

As Dustu rushed off with Waya, Awinita stood with Adahy watching the swiftly oncoming dark sky. "Awinita, can you check our supplies and be sure that everything is tied down? We might be in for a rough ride."

Just then the dolphins broke through the surface of the water, "Marco says there's a bad storm coming. We'll have to stay mostly under the water. He says he'll try to pull you away from it, but he's not sure if he can … he says it looks like a pretty big storm. He says to secure your boat because the high waves will most certainly wash over the deck."

"Thanks," Adahy answered them. "We're on it."

"Good luck," the dolphins worriedly wished them as they disappeared under the waves.

The wind picked up as Adahy unlashed the rope at the railing and brought it inside. Waya and Dustu had closed and securely latched the windows. Awinita closed the bins and tucked things on the shelves back as far as possible. Only the two doors remained open to let in some light.

The sky was now ominously dark, and the waves were becoming rougher. The ark began rocking back and forth and up and down as the angry water tossed it. Waya closed and latched the doors. Now it was very dark inside.

The boat suddenly lurched and Dustu lost his balance and fell to the deck. "Let's get into the hammocks," Awinita suggested, "Maybe that way we won't get hurt."

"Good idea," Waya agreed.

They each climbed into their hammocks which began to swing from side to side as the boat began to pitch more violently. "I sure hope we don't get sick," Adahy warned. "Fairies don't usually get motion sickness, but this may be too much for us."

At that moment the bow of the ship lifted high and then slammed down hard. Everyone screamed! Then the ark tilted violently to one side. Again everyone screamed!

"We're tipping over!" Awinita shrieked as she held tightly onto her wildly swinging hammock.

"Have faith!" Waya called out to her.

The waves and rain beat against the hull like great monsters trying to get inside. The ship rose and plunged down, over and over again.

"We're going under!" Dustu screamed over the sound of the howling wind.

"No! We are NOT!" Waya called out. "This ark is the same as Noah's ark, just a bit smaller. His boat survived the great flood because it was designed by the Creator, and so we will survive as well!"

They were in nearly total darkness, but Awinita could barely make out Dustu's terrified face—his eyes wide with fear. "Did you hear Waya? We're going to be OK!" she tried to reassure him, even while doubting ... she couldn't help it—she was so afraid.

Their boat violently lurched again, and one of the doors suddenly popped open! A great wave flooded across the deck and water swooshed inside! Waya and Adahy leapt from their hammocks and rushed to the door. As they tried to close it, the wind-driven rain soaked them and forced them backwards. Then the door at the other end of the room popped open as well! The ferocious wind again swept in with great force, bringing in more sea water.

"I'll take care of this one! You get the other!" Waya yelled out over the roar of the wind and waves.

Adahy turned and ran to the other door and tried to close it, but the wind was too fierce. He forced the door with all his strength, but as soon as he got it partially closed, the wind would gust and blow it open again, pushing him back.

Awinita clutched her hammock with all her strength as her worried eyes darted quickly between Adahy and Waya.

As Adahy fought his door, Waya was losing the battle with his. Another great wave crashed over the rails and washed inside, knocking Waya off his feet. Dustu rolled out of his hammock and rushed to Waya's aid. "No!' Waya warned, "Boy, go back!"

"But I can help!" Dustu insisted as he ran up and pushed against the door with Waya.

Adahy, with a strong push, finally got his door closed and latched. He hoped it would hold. Then he flew to help Waya and Dustu. Before he reached them, another powerful wave washed in and then out as the boat dipped. To Adahy's horror, both Waya and Dustu were swept away! Awinita screamed and leapt out of her hammock, only to be thrown to the deck as the boat lurched violently.

Adahy reached the open door and tightly held on as the deck pitched. He anxiously looked out. Through the heavy rain he saw great mountains of dark water rising high and then violently crashing down into the deep valleys they formed. Lightning flashed across the dark angry sky, briefly lighting up everything. As his eyes quickly searched the deck he saw Waya, but not Dustu! Waya was against the railing and leaning out over it. Then to Adahy's amazement, Waya climbed over the rail, spread his wings, and disappeared downward!

"No!" Adahy yelled. "Your wings are too wet to fly!"

Adahy heard Marco calling out, but couldn't make sense of it. He let go of the doorway and staggered out onto the lurching deck. A wave crashed into him and he lost his footing. He fell down and slid to the railing! He quickly grabbed onto the vertical slats as the water swished through them and back into the sea. He tightly held on and searched the violent waves below. There they were! Dustu and Waya! In the water, fighting to stay afloat! Adahy scrambled to his feet and yelled out to them, "I'm going to throw you the rope!"

He dashed back across the deck and into the room, grabbed the rope, and staggered back out as quickly as he could. He fell once when the deck dropped down from under him as the boat dipped, then he scrambled to his feet and ran to the rail closest to Waya and Dustu below. Tying the rope as quickly as he could, he looking frantically back and forth from his tying to the water. He jerked the rope to test his knot and then tossed it over the side. He leapt up and over the rail, held onto the rope, and slid down.

Waya and Dustu were so close! Waya was desperately trying to hold Dustu's head out of the water, while trying not to let himself drown. They both were sputtering and coughing as the water washed over them. It was amazing that they were still there, because fairies can't swim.

"Reach out!" Adahy yelled to them as he clung to the rope and stretched his arm out as far as he could. Waya, struggling desperately, forced Dustu toward Adahy's anxious hand. Adahy grabbed Dustu's outstretched arm and pulled. Waya had hold of Dustu's clothing, so Adahy's muscles bulged as he pulled them both toward himself. Then a wave reared up and covered all three of them. Adahy held tightly to Dustu's arm, but when the wave subsided, Waya was gone.

"No!" Adahy yelled over the roar of the ocean. "Waya! Waya!"

Adahy searched the tumultuous water as Dustu, coughing out seawater, clung to him. "Waya!" he continued to call out.

Awinita had managed to make it to the railing above them, and collapsed to her knees as she took in the scene below. Waya was gone.

He was gone.

Adahy waited, searching across the waves, hoping against hope to see Waya. Finally, he tried to flutter his wings, but they were just too wet for him to fly. He told Dustu to hold onto him as he began to climb the rope. When he reached the top, he nearly fell over the rail with exhaustion. With a final desperate search across the waves, he grabbed Dustu and Awinita into his arms and fought the forceful wind and ocean spray as it tried to knock them down. Finally, the three of them managed to stagger back inside and secure the door.

Chapter 15

Good-bye

The storm was finally over. The sun was rising to show clear sky. No one spoke as Adahy and Awinita opened the windows one by one. Dustu remained balled up in his hammock, unmoving. Adahy opened both doors to let more sunshine in, and then he walked out onto the deck. He continued around the center structure to see if he could find any damage, then he flew to the roof to inspect that as well. All thankfully seemed well and as he turned to fly off the roof, he saw a group of—what appeared to be—"heads" swimming toward the ark. As they got closer, he could see that they were some sort of sea people. They seemed to have something they were bringing with them. Marco's head broke the surface of the water nearby. The approaching sea people nodded respectfully toward him, but kept swimming toward the ark. Then Adahy could see what they were bringing— it was the body of Waya.

Awinita joined Adahy at the railing and then gasped when she saw Waya. "Oh, no," she moaned sadly, her voice breaking.

Marco thought to the fairies, "These are the People of the Sea. I had called them during the storm, hoping they could help us ..." his thoughts trailed off in sadness. Then he continued, "I wish I could have helped more, but I dared not get too close to the boat, because if I had been slammed against it, it would have broken up and sunk. I'm so sorry."

By then the People of the Sea had nearly reached the ark. Awinita and Adahy watched as they swam closer. They had grayish skin and tails like the dolphins, but also had arms and hands—with webbed fingers. The Sea People at the front of the group carried Waya, and those who followed had spears clutched in their hands.

Dustu had crept out of the doorway to see what was going on, but when he looked over the railing and saw the limp body of Waya, he let out an agonized wail of sorrow and ran back inside. He didn't even notice the Sea People.

Awinita turned to go after him, but he had slammed the door shut. She hesitated, and realized that he needed to be alone for a while—to grieve. She turned back to the Sea People below. They were conversing with Marco, "We came as soon as we heard your call," the fierce-looking leader of the group told him. "We found this strange body sinking toward the bottom, and we thought maybe that's why you called us."

"Yes," Marco explained, "I had hoped that you could have helped. These are my friends, fairies from a distant land, and the storm had washed the young one into the water. Fairies can't swim, but Waya ..." he glanced toward the limp form they carried, "flew down to try to save the young one." Marco's gaze shifted up toward the deck, "Adahy managed to catch the boy and save him, but the storm pulled Waya under. The boy looked up to Waya as a father figure and best friend. This is a great tragedy."

The sea people leader thought to Adahy, "Summon the young one, I wish to speak to him."

Puzzled, Adahy did as the leader wished. He walked over and opened the door. "Dustu," he called gently. "The sea people want to talk to you."

Dustu turned in his hammock, "What? What sea people?"

"Come on," Adahy encouraged. "Come and see."

Dustu rolled out of his hammock and sadly walked up to Adahy. His eyes were rimmed in red from his tears. Adahy put his arm around Dustu's shoulder and together they walked to the railing. Dustu was surprised to see the strange people in the water below.

As soon as the leader of the sea people saw him, he thought to Dustu, "Young one, we know that you grieve—but also know this. The brave one" he nodded toward Waya, "died for a friend—there is no greater honor than this. After the time of grieving then comes the time of honor. Honor him!" All the sea people who had spears raised them and repeated, "Honor him!" Then the leader thought to Adahy, "We would be pleased to take the brave one and lay him to rest among our warriors."

Adahy knew they couldn't take Waya's body with them, so he nodded to the leader, "Thank you for your kindness. We would be most pleased to have our friend with your people."

Several sea people disappeared under the water but soon returned with long stands of seaweed. They quickly and skillfully wrapped Waya's body tightly in the seaweed. When they were finished, the leader thought and said out-loud in their language to everyone, "Wish this brave one's spirit a swift journey back to the Creator!" Then all the sea people raised their voices, "Swift Journey!"

Adahy and Awinita bowed their heads, and said, "Good-bye, Waya."

Dustu's eyes brimmed with tears, as he choked out, "Good-bye Waya."

Most of the sea people instantly disappeared under the water, with Waya. The leader raised his spear and thought to Adahy, "We will protect you as you journey to the land. Marco had told us earlier of your quest to find the Savior. This is honorable. We will assist in any way that we can."

Surprised at the generous offer, Adahy answered, "Thank you! We will be most grateful for your help."

"Yes," Awinita thought to them and bowed her head, "and thank you ... for Waya."

The leader bowed his head back in acknowledgement. Then he disappeared beneath the sea.

Chapter 16

Land!

Dustu was bitter. He frowned all the time and barely spoke. He was angry that Waya had been taken from him. First his father had died in the great fire, and now Waya—the closest person he knew who acted like a new father to him.

Both Awinita and Adahy were concerned. That evening, Awinita sat next to Dustu on the deck and put her arm around his shoulders. "I'm worried about you," she said gently.

"Harrumph," he grunted back.

"Come on, Dustu, Waya wouldn't want you to be so sad all the time."

"Well, he's not here to tell me that, is he?" Dustu replied sarcastically.

Awinita sighed, "No, he isn't. I wish he were. We don't always know why things happen the way they do …"

"I do! The Creator let him drown. He could have saved him!" Then Dustu murmured bitterly, "I hate Him."

Awinita looked at him, aghast, "No, no, don't hate Him! We don't always know the 'why' and all the answers for what happens, but hating the Creator is just wrong!"

"I don't care," Dustu muttered. Then he turned to Awinita and questioned angrily, "But why did the Creator take him? Why didn't He let Waya be saved like I was?"

"I don't know," Awinita shook her head sadly, but then brightened, "Maybe when we find Jesus, we can ask Him!"

Dustu's face lit up as he remembered the story of Jesus raising a little girl from death, "Yeah! Maybe He'll bring Waya back to us! Just like in the story that the little bird told us!"

Awinita was overjoyed to see the change in Dustu, but feared that his hope would be a false one. "Dustu, don't get your hopes up for that. He might not ... "

Dustu interrupted her, "He can bring Waya back from the dead! He can, right?"

"Well, yes," she hesitated. "He *can* do anything, but I just don't want you to be disappointed if He doesn't ..."

Dustu nodded his head, ignoring her, "He *will* bring Waya back to us. I know He will."

*

The next day, two seagulls landed on the roof of the ark. Seeing the wings of the fairies, one called out, "Hey there, strange birds. Where do you come from?"

The other seagull eyed them suspiciously and squawked at them, "Got any food?"

Adahy put his fists on his hips and looked sternly at them, "No, we don't have any food, and we are *not* birds; we're fairies from a distant land."

Then another seagull landed on the roof, "Hey, you're fairies, aren't you?"

Adahy nodded to him, and replied, "Yes, have you seen our kind before?"

"Sure I have," then he cocked his head and said slyly, "And they gave us food. You'll give us food too, right?"

The others stared at Adahy eagerly, "Food! Yes, yes!"

Suddenly Marco's thoughts boomed out at them, "Seagulls, how far from land are we?"

The gulls leaned back when they saw Marco's great dark hulk rise from the water. "Uh, wow, you sure are big!"

Marco repeated, "I asked you, how far from land are we?"

The sly bird narrowed his eyes and asked, "If we tell you, will you give us food?"

Adahy rolled his eyes, but Marco said, "Yes, I'll provide lots of fish for you, but you must tell me first … and be accurate."

"OK, OK," the birds eagerly answered. "Land is not far. If the fairy-birds stand on top of the roof here, they should be able to see the land in a day or so. It's not much farther at all. Now, Mister Big, how about our fish?"

Without further conversation, Marco dove down into the depths. When he didn't immediately re-surface, the seagulls became impatient. "Where's our fish!" they demanded. "We're going to poop all over your fancy boat if you don't give us our fish!" The sly one raised his tail threateningly and Adahy immediately fluttered his wings, rising to chase the birds off the roof. Suddenly Marco surfaced and blew air, water … and small fish up into the air!

"Our fish!" the seagulls exclaimed as they launched themselves off the roof and eagerly flew over to catch the fish before they fell back into the sea. "I wish I had several beaks!" one thought wishfully as he snagged one. "So I could catch more! Thank you, Mister Giant Fish … may I sit on your back as I enjoy this feast?"

"Me too!" the other two seagulls eagerly asked, with their beaks each full with a struggling fish.

"Alright," Marco sighed. "I'll just dive down to rinse off the mess when you're done."

*

The next day was cloudy, but the following morning dawned clear and bright, and sure enough—the seagulls had spoken the truth. In the far distance, the fairies could see the faint shapes of what appeared to be land. Marco was amazed to discover that they had traveled farther than he had thought. "Must have had more of a tail current than I realized," he mused.

The dolphins surfaced and rejoiced with Marco and the fairies. But then Marco warned them that the journey was far from over. The land ahead was a wonderful sign, but they would still have to travel the vast inland sea to the land where Jesus would be. It would require another week of travel, and would be much more perilous because human ships traveled those waters.

The next day the leader of the sea people rose from the depths and called to the fairies, "Be warned! We are going to pass through the opening into the sea where the Roman ships travel. If they come too close—close enough to see your boat—we will then lead them away. Whenever they see us," he explained to the fairies, "they try to catch us. They call us 'mermaids.' They foolishly think that we are all females and that we lure sailors into the sea to eat them, or whatever," the leader said disgustedly. "Some think of our existence as myth. To capture one of us would be of great value to them, so they will chase us if we show ourselves. You must keep watch for the Roman ships, and we will as well." Then the leader slipped silently under the water.

"Thank you!" Adahy and Awinita called after him, but he had already disappeared.

"Not much for chit-chat, are they?" Adahy grinned to Awinita.

"I guess not, but I sure am glad they're here." Awinita smiled. "We're going to need their help."

Chapter 17

Captured!

They traveled through the Straits of Gibraltar into the Mediterranean Sea. They slipped through at night because the land was so close on both sides of the ark and they didn't want to risk being seen. Now, because they were no longer in open sea, Adahy and Dustu kept continual watch from the roof. So far, they saw some ships in the distance, but not close enough to them to cause alarm.

They were out of dried greens to eat, so as they were passing land on the port (left) side of the ark, they discussed the need for fresh food. Marco couldn't help much except to bring the boat as near to shore as possible. The dolphins swam the closest to the land, looking for the least human populated areas. The land was called Spain, and in many places ships were busily traveling. But also in some places there were vast forests—with no people.

When the ark was near a quiet forested coastline, Adahy and Dustu rode Binka and Finn toward the shore. Then they lifted off the dolphins and flew over the small sandy beach and into the wooded area. Awinita waited anxiously on the boat for their safe return. After several hours, she happily saw the bobbing heads of the dolphins coming toward her—with their riders. She leaned over the rail and waved to them.

"We got a lot of great stuff!" Dustu called up to her.

"We sure did!" Adahy agreed. "We got nuts, greens, some rose-hips, and even some berries!"

"Oh, that's so wonderful!" She clapped her hands together (she was tired of eating nothing but fish for the last few weeks.)

Adahy lifted the heavy grass and vine woven bag into his arms and fluttered his wings to fly up to the deck. "Wait for me to come back, Dustu," he called down to the boy, "and I'll get your bag."

"No, I can lift it," Dustu called back, as he struggled to lift the stuffed bag into his arms. He stood up on Finn's head and fluttered his wings, but he got no lift—his load was too heavy.

"I said wait!" Adahy called down to him again.

"I can do this!" Dustu insisted. He tried to fly again, but nearly lost his balance on Finn's head. Fearing the water, he dropped his bag and it splashed down into the sea! He flew up and tried to retrieve it from the waves as it began to sink. "No!" he yelled out in frustration.

"I'll get it," Finn thought to him calmly.

Finn's head disappeared under the water and immediately came back up with the bag balanced on his nose. Adahy flew down and gathered the wet bag into his arms, then he flew back up to the deck. Dustu flew up with Adahy and landed next to him.

"Why didn't you do like I said?" Adahy scolded the boy. "The bag was too heavy for you when we left the shore; so did you think it would suddenly become lighter when we got to the boat?"

Dustu hung his head. "I guess not," he mumbled.

Adahy sighed and then said, "Dustu, sometimes we need help to do the thing we want. We can't always do everything by ourselves. Plus we have to realize our limitations. You're a boy now, but you *will* become a man, and then you'll be able to do the things that you can't now. Understand?"

Dustu nodded.

Adahy knew he could never take the place of Waya, but he was trying to do the best he could to be a good mentor for the boy. Awinita came up to them and put her delicate arms around both of them, changing the subject, "I'm so glad that you are both home safely. And, what a wonderful haul you've brought!"

"Dustu found the nuts!" Adahy praised the boy.

"Oh, how marvelous!" Awinita praised him as well. "We'll have a feast tonight, won't we?" she smiled as she squeezed Dustu's shoulders.

Dustu grinned up to her, "Yes, and I found some really fat rose-hips for you!"

"That's terrific!" she smiled and then kissed the top of her brother's head. "Tell you what, let's make dinner right now!"

*

After the feast, they all sat on the deck watching the sun set. Suddenly Dustu let out a loud rolling burp. Adahy grinned and said, "Better out than in, right kid?"

Awinita just rolled her eyes and muttered, "Men!"

Just then, one of the sea people raised his head from the waves and thought-called to the fairies, "Friends, there are several Roman ships heading into our path ahead!"

Adahy, Dustu, and Awinita immediately went to the rail. "How far?" Adahy called back.

"Ahead!" the young sea-man answered. "Marco will slow his tow of your boat, and I will lead the Romans away."

"Thank you," Adahy called back, "Please be careful!"

"As always," he answered, and disappeared under the water.

Adahy flew up to keep watch from the roof, and he soon saw the Roman ships in the distance. There were two together, and the third followed at a distance.

Then Binka's head broke the surface of the water. "The young sea-man wanted me to tell you and Marco that he is going to let the Romans see him and chase him. Finn, Tinka, and Chipper are going to travel along with him to see how it goes."

"Thank you, Binka, please keep us informed," Adahy called back to her. The dolphin nodded her head and slipped back into the sea.

Minutes passed, and passed, while the fairies nervously waited. Suddenly Finn leapt up from the water and splashed back down. "They caught him!" he exclaimed frantically. "The Romans captured the sea-man with nets! There was nothing we could do!"

The other dolphins were right behind Finn. "What do we do!" they anxiously asked. "We have to find the other sea-people and tell them!"

Marco surfaced near them and offered, "I can go and give their ship a bump, if that would help."

"No," Finn shook his head. "They would shoot you full of their sharp arrows, and the sea-man would still be caught!"

"Maybe I can help!" Adahy interrupted. "I can get aboard their ship and try to rescue him!"

"What?" Marco asked. "How do you figure that?"

"I can make myself invisible and get aboard and try! The Roman people won't see me!"

"You can make yourself *invisible*?" Finn asked incredulously.

"Yes, it's a gift all fairies have."

"Well, you are just *full* of surprises," Marco marveled.

"Now," Adahy continued, "if Finn can give me a lift to the ships, I can remain invisible and then fly up onto their deck and try to find the sea-man. I'll take my knife to cut the net. How long can he remain out of water?"

A voice from the sea answered, "Not long. His skin will dry out and he will die." Adahy saw the leader of the Sea People swimming to the ark, along with a large group of his warriors. "The one they caught is my son, and we are here to fight for him."

"We can all go, but let me try to get to him first, before there's a battle," Adahy said, fearing loss of his new friends' lives.

"I'm going too!" Dustu announced.

"No," Awinita began to object. "You're too young ..."

"We might need the young warrior's help," the Sea People leader interrupted, "if he can become invisible as well."

Dustu instantly disappeared and then reappeared.

The fierce-looking leader gasped in surprise and then said, "Ah, very impressive. If you both are ready, let us proceed."

Helpless, Awinita watched Adahy and Dustu fly down to the waiting heads of Finn and Binka. "Be careful!" she called to them as they quickly swam away.

*

About half way to the Roman ships, Adahy and Dustu turned themselves invisible. The ships were very large and had great colorfully striped sails billowing in the wind. The dolphins swam close to the backs of the ships, and then Adahy and Dustu flew off their heads. They invisibly flew to the deck of the great ship, which had captured the sea-man, and squatted down.

"Now, what?" Dustu whispered to Adahy.

"Now," Adahy whispered back, "you stick with me. We'll search the upper deck here first. Stay close to the railing."

The two of them crept along, not realizing that they were leaving wet footprints.

Suddenly a loud deep voice thundered, "What foolishness is this?" Alarmed, Adahy and Dustu darted closer to the ship's railing and looked behind them. A big Roman officer was peering at the deck. "Now elves?" he bellowed. "First mermaids, now imps? Ridiculous! Who made these footprints?"

The soldiers who were following him stared in disbelief at the quickly drying little footprints. "Sir," one answered, "We know nothing of this. Are we cursed?"

"Ha!" the big man laughed loudly. "Superstitious fools. Now, where is this so-called *mermaid* that you claim you caught?"

"This way, sir. We tied him near the bow."

Adahy and Dustu looked at each other. Then they both fluttered their wings and flew up and toward the bow—the front of the ship—as fast as they could. They got there before the men, and were horrified to see the young sea-man covered in a net, grimacing in pain.

Adahy landed and immediately began cutting the net with his knife. In spite of his pain, the young sea-man's eyes grew wide as he saw a piece of the netting rise off him—as if by magic. "Wh … what?" he thought. Seeing his shock, Adahy became visible and then Dustu did as well. "Oh," he gasped, "My friends! I'm … how did you get here?"

"No time to explain," Adahy said, furiously sawing at the net. "The Romans are coming." The net separated and Adahy began to cut the next piece. He looked at the fish-type tail the young man had, and asked, "When you're free, can you crawl with your arms to the rail and lift yourself over it?"

"Yes, I think so, just please hurry cutting me free. My skin is so dry …"

"I'll get some water," Dustu quickly offered, and then flew up and over the side of the ship. He was back in a moment with a double handful of water … and a mouthful. He dumped the small handful on the sea-man's head and spit the rest onto his body. Then he leapt up and flew over the rail again for more.

The Romans were almost upon them. Adahy pulled on the last cut he had made and the net separated enough for the sea-man to wriggle out. Dustu arrived just in time to dump some more water onto the young man and spit the rest onto his belly. Then the sea-man frantically began to "swim" across the deck, pulling his body with his arms and pushing with his tail toward the railing.

One of the Roman soldiers saw him and yelled out as he ran forward, "It's getting away!"

The sea-man desperately pulled himself up to the railing. Adahy and Dustu grabbed the small fins on the sea-man's side and tried with all their strength to help heave him up and over the rail. Finally, with one last push, the sea-man slipped over and splashed down into the sea!

Adahy and Dustu turned to see that the Roman soldier was upon them! "Go!" Adahy shouted, and they both became invisible.

The Roman soldier stood there with his mouth hanging open. He had just seen two small winged creatures help a mermaid into the sea.

"Well?" the loud Roman officer bellowed from behind him. "Where's your mermaid?"

The soldier gulped and said nervously, "Sir, it got away."

"So, it got away, did it?" the officer growled, placing his fists on his hips. "Didn't you tie it up securely?"

"Yes, sir, I did ... but it had help getting free," he answered, miserably.

"So, who helped it?"

"Uh, sir, a couple of elves ... or something ... got it free."

"What!" the officer roared. "Elves? Do you think I have time for your jokes? Off to the brig!"

Chapter 18

Wise One

As soon as the young sea-man flopped over the rail and splashed into the water, the Sea People were there to greet him. The leader gave his son a quick hug, but then scolded him for going alone to lead the Romans away. Dustu and Adahy, still invisible, flew back to Binka and Finn, and then together they all swam back to the ark.

The Sea People were very grateful for the successful rescue of the leader's son. They assured the fairies that they would continue to help them avoid Roman ships, which was even more important because they were nearing the coast of Israel.

*

Chipper joined the other dolphins frequently. The leader of the Sea People asked him if he knew where a good place would be to hide the ark. He didn't know, but he knew someone who would—an old pelican—the Wise One. So, he swam ahead to try to locate the wise pelican, who—on most days—sat on an old stump that stuck out of the water within the harbor. He knew that the Wise

One would remember the location of the docking area where Joseph, the father of Jesus (that's who everyone thought he was) built the ark. After carefully dodging many small fishing boats in the active harbor, he swam up to the weathered stump. Perched there was the Wise One, keeping watch on the busy comings and goings.

"Uh, hello, sir," Chipper greeted the old pelican politely.

"Hey, sonny," Wise One replied. "What are you doing so close to shore? It's dangerous here, you know. Someone might mistake you for a fat fish and try to catch you for dinner."

"Yes, sir, I'll be careful," Chipper nodded. "I came here to ask if you know where a boat was made some years ago by Joseph of Nazareth."

"Hummm," Wise One squinted his eyes, remembering. "Yes, I do remember. He was making a boat to carry some of the fairy people to a distant land, as I recall."

"Oh, that's great sir!" Chipper exclaimed. "Other fairies have sailed from that distant land back across the great sea, and they need to hide the boat while they visit here."

"I see," mused Wise One. "The place where Joseph and his friend constructed the ark still stands, and his friend still makes boats there. However, I have sad news to tell you. Word came that Joseph died a few years back—not long after he finished the boat and returned to his wife, Mary, in Nazareth."

"Oh, I'm so sorry to hear that," Chipper said quietly.

"Yes, we were too," Wise One shook his head sadly. "He was a good man—the best, as humans go." Wise One paused and then continued, "But enough of sad news, follow me to that boat-building warehouse." Wise One spread his large wings and gracefully lifted off his stump and began to fly.

Chipper followed the pelican to a rickety old pier. When Wise One saw Chipper's head break the surface of the water, he nodded his head toward the pier. "See inside there?"

Chipper forced himself a bit out of the water so he could get a better view. Through the open doors of a large old wooden building, he could see a man working on an upside-down rowboat.

"That man is the friend of Joseph," Wise One said. "We can't talk to him, as you know, so you'll have to get one of the fairies to come. He shouldn't be shocked to see them because he knew the other fairies for whom they built the ark."

"Thank you so much, sir. May I find a nice fish for you because you helped me?" Chipper asked respectfully.

"Thank you, sonny, but helping others requires no reward."

"Tell that to the seagulls," Chipper muttered.

Wise One rolled his eyes, "Yes, I too don't understand their greed. Kindness and helpfulness should be given freely, not with expectations of rewards. So, sonny, I wish you well." Then the kind old pelican rose up and flew back to his stump.

Chipper returned to the open sea to find his waiting fairy and dolphin friends. He swam up to the ark. "Hey, topside!" he called up.

Within a few moments Adahy leaned over the rail. "Chipper! Good to see you! What did you find out?"

"Good news! The place where this boat was built is still there, and looks to be a great place to dock safely. But, one of you needs to come ashore and talk to the human who owns that pier."

"Just a moment," Adahy thought-called down to Chipper. "I'll be right back." Adahy left the rail to go speak to Awinita. "I need to go ashore to speak with someone who can help us hide our boat. I shouldn't be gone long. Will you be OK?"

"Of course, Adahy," Awinita smiled up to him. "Dustu and I will be fine. Just hurry back, if you can," she said with confidence, but inwardly wished he didn't have to go.

Just then Dustu ran over to them. "Where're you going? I want to go too!"

"Not this time, buddy," Adahy said, ruffling Dustu's hair. "Stay here and be the 'Captain of the Ship.'"

"Does that mean I get to boss my sister around?"

"No," Awinita said firmly. "It does not."

Dustu frowned with mock disappointment, and Adahy laughed. "I'll be back soon. Be good."

From the water came a thought-voice, "We will accompany you." The fairies went and leaned over the rail. Below was the Sea People leader. His son and several others then broke through the water's surface, joining him. "We will assure your safety."

*

Adahy, invisible, rode on Chipper's head as they carefully entered the busy harbor. The Sea People escort swam close by, keeping a sharp eye on the many boats there. Chipper swam slowly to the pier where the middle-aged human worked. Adahy fluttered his wings and flew from Chipper to the pier. He made himself visible as he walked through the wide-open doors, unnoticed.

"Excuse me," Adahy said quietly. The man continued at his work. "Excuse me!" Adahy announced himself more loudly.

The man looked down and saw a small, winged, pointed-ear creature standing there before him. "Ah!" he exclaimed, startled. Then he peered more carefully at Adahy and remembered, "Oh! You're one of the fairy people!"

"Yes, sir. My name is Adahy. I understand that you helped Joseph of Nazareth make an ark for some of my kinsmen—people of my kind."

"Oh my, yes," he nodded his head happily. "They were on a quest to tell the world's creatures of Jesus, the one Son of God."

"Yes, sir, they came to our village on a distant land across the great sea, and some of us have returned to find Him and learn and share His teachings."

"Wonderful," the man clapped his hands together. "That means the ark we made for them arrived safely!"

"Yes, sir, and it safely returned back to this land with us. But we have a problem. We need to hide it until we leave to return to our home."

"That is not going to be a problem for you, my small friend. You may dock it right here, at my pier. No one will bother it, I assure you."

Just then the man saw strange heads poking up from the water. He clasped at his heart and staggered backward, gasping in fear, "Demons!"

Adahy turned to see some of the Sea People. "Oh, no sir, they're not demons at all. The Sea People are our friends," he reassured the man. "They have helped us arrive here safely."

The Sea People leader, hearing Adahy's thoughts, was incensed. "Demons!" he sneered. "If he wants to see demons, just look to the humans who hunt us! What a load of whale poop. I wish he could hear me, I'd tell him what to do with his 'demon' comments!"

Adahy, hearing the sea-man's angry words while he was trying to talk to the man, was having a hard time not laughing.

The man's wide open eyes still stared at the strange beings in the water. He shook his head and said with wonder, "God's many creations are truly marvelous, indeed. Please express my apology to your strange friends."

Adahy nodded and turned to the sea-men, thinking to them, "The human is sorry for insulting you. He just had never seen any of your people before. He asks that you accept his apology."

Frowning, the sea-man raised his spear and nodded curtly, then he and the others disappeared beneath the water.

Chapter 19

Mister Jericho

Adahy returned to the ark and gave the good news to Awinita and Dustu. He and the man, who was named Jericho, had decided that the best time to move the ark into the harbor would be late at night. Jericho said that he would construct a floating platform on which to put an oil lamp, and tie it to the end of his pier. Any other lights in the harbor would be above the water, so finding his dock in the dark should be easy.

Marco could not enter the harbor—it was far too dangerous for him. He said that he would go krill hunting for a while, and then come back when he got word that the fairies would need his services again to return to their far-away homeland. The fairies profusely thanked Marco for his great kindness in helping them, and were sorry to see him leave.

They waited for night, and when it was very dark, the dolphins all gathered together and tugged on the straps—slowly pulling the boat into the harbor. Very few people were up at that late hour, so they silently glided unseen past the many tied-up boats. The plan worked perfectly. When they arrived, Mister Jericho tied the ark against his pier next to the protected area of his warehouse. Adahy and Awinita thanked the dolphins over and over. The dolphins said that they would go to the sea until they received word from the seagulls to return.

Dustu slept through it all.

*

The next morning dawned sunny and bright. Dustu was up early, but Adahy and Awinita slept for a while longer—they were still tired from being up most of the night. Dustu made himself invisible and went out onto the deck. He looked all about in wonderment. The ark was tied right up against an old pier. He peered over the rail to the water below. It was dark—almost black—and had stuff floating in it—like trash.

He heard a strange noise—like a saw chewing through wood. He fluttered his wings and flew over to the wooden floor-planks of the pier. It was odd ... the long side of the building was open to the water, but the ends of the building on the pier had locked doors. He quietly walked further in toward the strange noise. In the far corner was a large bed, and upon that bed was a human man—sound asleep. *He* was the source of the racket—snoooog ... pshuuu, snoooog ... pshuuu, snoooog ... pshuuu. Dustu crept closer. Each time the man snored, his long grey beard lifted and dropped. Dustu flew up onto the edge of the bed. He was very curious about the man's beard—he had never seen one before.

Suddenly the man moved. Startled, Dustu fluttered up and forgot to keep himself invisible. He was knocked a bit by the shifting blanket that covered the man, and he landed on the man's chest.

Jericho woke with a shock. "Ahhheeek!" both the man and boy shrieked. Dustu scrambled backwards and the man sat up. Horrified, they stared at each other.

Then the man smiled, "So, you are a fairy child!"

"Y ... Yes, sir," Dustu trembled. "I ... I'm sorry I woke you."

"No problem at all, young one. I needed to get up anyway. A new day has begun!" Mr. Jericho stretched and then turned to Dustu, "How about something to eat?"

*

Awinita and Adahy woke to find Dustu missing. They called out for him but got no answer. Alarmed, Adahy lifted Awinita into his arms and flew to the pier. Then they heard Dustu's laughter coming from the building. Relieved, they walked across the pier and found Mister Jericho sharing his breakfast with Dustu.

Awinita and Adahy joined them and enjoyed cooked grain and fruit. Mister Jericho suggested that after breakfast, they go to the merchant piers where they could find a ride to the nearby town. There, they might find news of a caravan traveling to Jerusalem, where Jesus was known to visit each year for the holy celebration of Passover.

Chapter 20

He Fed the Multitudes

So, the fairies (Adahy carrying Awinita) flew over to the busy merchant piers. There people bought merchandise from the incoming ships, or brought their wares to be shipped to other places. It was very busy, so the fairies had to be careful. They perched on top of a pier railing and listened to the many conversations that overlapped each other. Finally they heard mention of the nearby town. It came from a merchant who bought a load of fish from a fishing vessel, and was loading it onto his cart that was pulled by two oxen.

Adahy flew over and settled on the back of another cart that was parked in front of the oxen. He thought-greeted the oxen, "Hello, there."

"Hello, fairy," one ox greeted back.

"So, you know of our kind?" Adahy asked.

"Of course we do," the first ox replied.

"We're not stupid, you know," the second ox added.

"Of course not, I did not mean to imply ..." Adahy tried to explain.

The first ox flicked his ear, chasing off a fly. "So, what's up? Why are you here?"

"My name is Adahy. May I speak with you for a moment?" Adahy requested politely.

"Sure," the first ox agreed. "My name is Bullox."

"It's a good thing that you are invisible to humans," the second ox said. "Humans don't take kindly to something that they can't or don't want to understand ... and my name is Brutus."

"I'm happy to meet you both. My friends and I, Awinita and Dustu, need a ride to the local town. Would you mind if we rode along with you?"

"No, we don't mind at all. But, you had better sit up here on us instead of on the cart, because that load of fish will stink. It's all fresh fish, but our master doesn't clean the cart very well and it stinks all the time."

"Thanks for the warning," Adahy smiled. "And thank you for the ride."

Adahy carried Awinita and the three of them settled on the backs of the oxen—Adahy and Awinita on Bullox and Dustu on Brutus. The owner of the oxen had finished his purchase of fish from the fishing boat, and the cart began to move. "Why do you need to go to town?" Bullox asked. "Not many fairies there."

"We're not going to visit our kind," Awinita explained. "We need to try to find a caravan that's going to Jerusalem. We are trying to locate Jesus of Nazareth."

"Oh, we have heard of Him!" Bullox exclaimed. "I heard that he made fish appear out of thin air!"

"Really?" Dustu asked.

"Oh, yes, He sure did. Our master would love it if he could make fish appear like Jesus did, so he wouldn't have to buy them.

We would love that too, because then we wouldn't have to pull this heavy cart!"

The fairies laughed, and then Dustu asked, "Can you tell us the story? About how Jesus made fish appear like magic?"

"Of course," Bullox said. "It happened several months ago ..."

"It was a year ago," Brutus interrupted.

"A year ago, then. Jesus had gone to a remote place, and great herds of people followed Him—more than five thousand men plus lots of women and kids. He taught them and healed their illnesses. It was getting late, but all the people had brought no food with them, so one of His friends told Him to send the people away to a nearby town. There they could buy food and find a place to sleep. Jesus told His men that they didn't need to go, and for His men to feed the people right there. But the men said that they couldn't because they didn't have any food either ..."

"Except for the boy," Brutus interrupted again.

"Who's telling this story?" Bullox demanded, irritated.

"Get it right, then," Brutus muttered.

"Except for a boy. He had five little loaves of bread and two fishes. Jesus told everyone to sit down on the grass. Then Jesus took the fishes and the bread and looked up into heaven and then blessed the food. Then He broke the bread and passed out the fishes, and guess what?" Bullox asked mischievously.

"What?" the fairies all asked together.

"As He passed out the bread and the fishes, neither the bread nor the fish ran out! He and His men kept passing out the food, and it never ran out! At the end of the dinner, they collected the scraps and filled baskets and baskets!"

"Twelve baskets full," Brutus interrupted again.

"Yes, twelve baskets full! Amazing, right?"

"But how is that even possible?" Dustu exclaimed.

"That's why it's called a miracle!"

"Truly amazing," the fairies agreed.

"And He did it again, I heard," Brutus added. "He did the same with another herd of people, this time over four thousand, and he fed them all with seven loaves of bread and several fishes, and when they were finished eating, they had seven baskets full of left-overs!"

"Incredible," they all agreed.

Chapter 21

The Market

The trip to the town took little time. The closer they got, the more activity they encountered. People were everywhere, busy going about their business. The town was noisy with children laughing, merchants calling out as they sold their wares, oxen-donkey-horse traffic, and strange music. There were odd smells as well—some nice and some not so nice. But the most fascinating were the bright colors everywhere! The gold tasseled vendor tents, the tinkling jewelry on the people, the fresh fruit and vegetables, and so much more!

Compared to the gentle forest sounds of home and the quiet of their long sea voyage, the excitement in the town was nearly overwhelming! But still, the fairies listened as they traveled, hoping to hear mention of a caravan—but they heard nothing.

The owner of the cart stopped at several shops to deliver his fish. When the cart was empty, he directed his oxen to pull the cart to his home at the edge of town. "You fairy people are welcome to stay the night in our barn, if you would like," Bullox offered.

"Thank you so much," Adahy answered gratefully. "I think we need to go back into town for a while and then we can come back here for the evening."

"That would be fine," Brutus agreed, as he stomped his hoof and chased a couple of flies away.

The fairies waved goodbye to their new friends. It was only early afternoon, so they had time to return to the town and listen for the latest news. Adahy scooped up Awinita and they all flew back to the busy market. They soon came to a fruit stand and landed on its colorful canopy-roof. Invisible, they watched as the fruit vendor bargained with his customers and then occasionally threw a damaged piece of fruit under the table and into a basket.

It was obvious that the cast-off fruit was unwanted by the merchant, but not by the fairies—it would make a nice lunch. So, they flew down and crept over to and then under the table. They wanted to gather some of the unwanted fruit and put them into the woven bags that they each carried.

Dustu picked up an oval dark brown fruit. "This is weird looking … it looks like those bugs that live in old wood!" Dustu grimaced and handed it to Awinita.

She took it carefully and looked it over. "It's not a bug," she murmured. Then she gingerly sniffed it. "It smells good," she nodded, and then took a small nibble of it. Her eyes widened as a smile curved her lips. "It's so sweet! What do you think it is?"

Adahy turned to look at it. "I heard a customer call it a 'dried date.'"

One of the vendor's customers held a small child in his arms. Seeing Dustu (children can often see things that adults cannot) the child bent over and stretched her arms out, calling "be-be," and fidgeted to be let down. The man, still bargaining with the fruit vendor, set the child onto her unsteady feet.

The grinning baby toddled toward the unsuspecting Dustu, who was now taking a big bite of the date. Her eyes gleamed with delighted eagerness as she reached out. Suddenly chubby arms surrounded Dustu. He shrieked in terror! "Aaaakk!" his voice cut off as the child's strong little arms squeezed him tightly.

"Be-Be!" the toddler squealed happily as she hugged him. Then she noticed Dustu's iridescent wings! Fascinated, she grabbed one with her fat little fingers and pulled it toward her open mouth.

Eyes wide in horror, Dustu squirmed violently to free himself. Thankfully, the baby's father saw his child under the table, so he reached down and picked her up. The baby nearly lost her grip on Dustu, but managed to hold onto him—dangling him upside down by his leg.

"Help!" Dustu screamed out, terrified. "A monster has me!"

In shock, Adahy and Awinita turned and gasped to see Dustu in the clutches of the human toddler! Dustu thrashed about and tried to whack the child's arm with his empty fruit bag. He managed to smack her arm once. The baby let out a wail and released him.

Free from the grip of his captor, Dustu fluttered his wings and fell to the ground. Frustrated, the baby leaned over and again tried to escape her father's arms. She reached downward and cried out for her former prey, "Me be-be! Me be-be!" Then, after a few more moments, the man thankfully walked away carrying his squirming child.

Now safely under the table, Dustu collapsed onto the ground. Adahy and Awinita rushed over to him and anxiously asked, "Are you all right? Did that child harm you?"

Dustu took a deep breath and answered, "I think I'm OK. That was a close one! I thought I was a goner!"

"We did too," Adahy said, shaking his head.

"Dustu," Awinita began, "human children can be dangerous because they don't understand what they're doing. You need to avoid them."

"Really?" Dustu rolled his eyes. "Do you think I wanted that kid to get me? She somehow saw me when I was invisible. How can that be? I hope I'm not getting sick or something."

"No, I doubt that," Awinita reassured him. "It's just that human babies can often see things that the adults cannot. Just be careful when the little ones are around."

"Not a problem," Dustu nodded his head. "Next time, if I see one coming, I'm outta there. Those creatures are dangerous!"

Chapter 22

We have a Ride!

After Dustu's terrifying experience, the fairies gathered some of the fruit from under the table and flew back up to the fruit vendor's tent roof. There they sat and enjoyed their lunch. It was becoming hotter as the afternoon passed, so they decided to fly to another place where there was some shade.

The new place belonged to a vendor of feed for animals. It was a larger tented area, with many bags of feed-grain in the back. The grain smelled very good, and Dustu flew down to investigate. He found quite a bit of spilled grain sprinkled all over the bags, so he gathered it and put it into his bag. He flew back to Adahy and Awinita who were talking together. "Hey!" he announced. "Look what I found!" He opened his bag and showed them the nice fresh grain.

"Dustu, you didn't steal this, did you?" Awinita asked, alarmed.

"No, of course not. It's spilled grain. There was lots of it on the ground, but this was spilled on the other bags, so it's clean."

"Good work, kid!" Adahy smiled. "Let's go check it out."

The fairies flew into the tent—invisible—and saw the many bags of grain, and the careless spills of it. They gathered as much as they could into their bags, and were about to leave when they heard voices coming toward them.

"Yes, I'll need all you have. And I'll take those other things up front," a customer said.

"How long of a trip will this be?" the merchant asked.

"All the way to Jerusalem, so I need to stock up," the customer answered.

"No problem. I'll deliver it to you tomorrow before evening, after I close up," the merchant promised happily as both men returned to the front of the shop.

"Did you hear that?" Adahy exclaimed. "We have a ride to Jerusalem! Let's get back to the oxen barn. We can sleep there tonight and then get a ride back to the docks in the morning. Tomorrow, we have to gather as many supplies as we can before the ox cart leaves the docks to return to this town. Then we can get a ride to the caravan on this merchant's delivery of the grain."

"Sounds like a good plan," Awinita smiled at Adahy as he gathered her up into his strong arms.

*

That evening they all fell asleep easily, but during the night, Awinita tossed and turned—she had another nightmare of the great fire. Adahy and Dustu were used to her nightmares so they did not wake up. But Bullox did, and he asked her about it the next morning. She explained what had happened and the oxen said they were sorry to hear about it.

The morning was bright, and they would be getting an early start traveling back to the docks. In no time at all, they were back at the harbor. The fairies thanked their friends for the ride and told them that they would be back for the return trip. Then they quickly flew to Mister Jericho's pier.

"Mister Jericho!" they called out when they arrived.

"Oh, my little friends!" he welcomed them. "I'm glad to see you back. I've heard of a large caravan that's going all the way to Jerusalem, and they'll arrive just before the Passover celebration."

"Yes, we heard of it too!" Dustu said eagerly.

"That's why we rushed back," Adahy added.

"And we need to gather some supplies, if we can," Awinita joined in.

"What do you need?" Mister Jericho asked.

"Food, mostly, and we need to fill our water skins," Awinita paused, and then continued, "It won't be enough for such a long trip, so I hope we can get more later."

"Look around here and take whatever you want," Mister Jericho offered. "If there is anything else you need, I'll try to get it for you right now."

The fairies thanked kind Mister Jericho for his generosity, and gathered as much as they could. Mister Jericho left for a little while and returned with some smoked fish to add to their packs. He told them not to worry about their ark, as he was planning to hoist is up out of the water and re-apply water sealant to the outer hull. Then, it would be ready for their return voyage back to their land across the great sea. He wished them a safe journey.

The fairies thanked Mr. Jericho again and then rushed back to the docks. They searched for the ox cart but did not see it! Then they heard some awful hollering in the distance. There they saw their oxen friends—who were refusing to pull the cart—with their very angry master! They quickly flew (not quite as fast as usual because of their load) to them.

"We're here!" Awinita called out.

"Finally!" Brutus muttered.

"Oh, we're glad to see you!" Bullox exclaimed. "Our master is furious with us. I was afraid he would whip us, but we decided that we would 'take it' until you got here."

"We're so sorry. We hurried as fast as we could," Adahy panted as he and Awinita landed onto their backs.

"Let's go," Brutus mumbled, "before our master has a stroke."

To the amazement of the cart owner, his fish-filled ox cart suddenly began moving forward. He stopped yelling at his oxen, wondering what had happened to make them go. He scratched his beard, puzzled, as they traveled toward the town.

Chapter 23

Caravan

Everything proceeded according to their plans. The fairies arrived in town and thanked Bullox and Brutus for their kind help. Then they waited at the animal-feed vendor's tent. Later, the vendor loaded up three donkey carts and started his trip to deliver the bags of grain to his customer at the caravan. The fairies rode together on the last cart.

The road was dusty and the late afternoon grew hotter. It was a miserable trip, and they were glad when they reached a large grove of palm trees. They saw that the caravan was gathered in the cool shade. There they saw many carts parked together. Oxen and donkeys grazed nearby ... along with some very large—and very strange—creatures that they had never seen before. They were tall with long necks plus they had a large hump on their backs.

Adahy scooped up Awinita and they all flew up to a low hanging palm branch. "I'm sorry to be such a burden ... because you have to carry me whenever we need to fly."

Adahy smiled at her and replied, "It's not a problem. In fact, carrying you is great exercise and has made me stronger." Adahy then flexed his arm muscles and expanded his wings. "See?" he grinned.

Awinita smiled and said, "You know what I mean."

Adahy smiled at her and said softly, "You are not a burden at all. You are light as a feather, and I enjoy helping you."

"You are always so kind." Awinita blushed, she just couldn't help it.

The fairies watched in awe from the palm branch above as more and more people with their animals and carts arrived. All of the human people seemed to be in good moods as evening arrived. They ate large dinners as they talked and laughed together. Then they played instruments and some of the women sang as they sat around the fires. All were in high spirits, because in the morning, their long trip to Jerusalem would begin.

*

The next morning, the Caravan leader loudly announced that everyone should prepare to leave. Most of the people were already up and finishing their breakfast. The fairies were doing the same. Adahy decided that they should try to ask for a ride toward the front of the assembling caravan because the dust wouldn't be so bad there. So, he flew to one of the strange animals in the lead and said, "Hello, sir," he thought-greeted politely. "May I have a word with you?"

"Yesss ... certainly," the animal with the hump answered.

"Please forgive me for asking, but what manner of animal are you?"

"Why, I'm a camel, of course ... have you never seen my kind before?" the old camel replied slowly, smacking his lips.

"No, sir," Adahy replied. "I never have ... but my friends and I are from a far-away land across the great sea."

112

"Really?" said the camel with surprise. "You are a long way from home, then."

"Yes, sir," Adahy explained. "We're on a journey, and my two companions and I very much need a ride to Jerusalem. We wondered if perhaps we might ride on your back?"

"Certainly ... but I don't know where my master is going ... he may go to Jerusalem ... or he may go somewhere else ... I never know ... I just carry him and his packs," the camel slowly spoke, then smacked his lips again.

"Well, in any case, thank you so much," Adahy nodded to him. "I'll go get the others."

Adahy hurriedly flew back to where Awinita and Dustu were waiting. "Found a ride! Let's go!" They gathered their things and Adahy lifted Awinita into his arms. They then flew to the waiting camel. They landed up on the camel's back and on top of his master's strapped-on packs. Between two of the packs there was a dip in which the fairies could safely ride—unseen.

Adahy called to the camel, "We're back!"

"You fairies had better stay invisible to humans ... until after my master gets on," the old camel suggested. "Oh ... here he comes now."

A gruff looking man walked up to the camel and tapped his front legs with a switch. "Hang on," the camel warned, "I have to get on my knees for him to climb up."

The camel leaned forward and then jerked as he bent his knees to the ground, then he jerked backward as his hind legs bent down as well. The fairies grabbed the pack-straps and tightly held on. The man struggled up and into the seat mounted upon the camel's back, and then he slapped his switch on the camel's side. The camel rocked back and forth again as he stood up.

"That's so hard ... on my knees," he sighed. "Are you little people OK?"

"Yes, sir," Adahy answered as the fairies hid themselves among the packs. "My name is Adahy."

"And mine is Dustu!"

"And I'm Awinita. We thank you so much for your help."

"You're very welcome," the camel nodded, "and my name is Gamal .... Why are you going ... to Jerusalem? It's such a long trip."

"We are going to find Jesus of Nazareth!" Dustu eagerly answered.

"Have you heard of Him?" Awinita asked.

"Yesss," the old camel smacked his lips. "I have indeed heard of the man called Jesus of Nazareth. In fact, I carried my master to a wedding several years ago .... Yesss, I remember. The very large number of wedding guests were quickly drinking up all the wine ... and getting a bit tipsy too, I might add .... So, I was standing out back, and I heard the mother of Jesus tell the servants to do whatever her Son told them to do .... It didn't make any sense to me, but I watched anyway."

Gamal paused, remembering, "So, Jesus told the servants to gather pots of water ... six of them as I recall ... and fill them to the tippy-top." Gamal smacked his lips again. "Then He told them to go to the wedding planner and let him taste the 'water.' The wedding planner tasted it and was very pleased ... Yesss, very pleased. He called to the groom ... the new husband, that is ... and complemented him because usually the best wine is brought out first for the wedding guests to drink ... then the cheaper wine is brought out later ... when they won't notice the difference .... But in this case, the very best wine was brought out last! Very unusual! The wedding planner didn't know he was drinking the fine wine that just a few minutes ago had been plain water! Haw! Haw!" old Gamal laughed. "But those people were rude."

"Why is that?" Dustu asked.

"Because they didn't offer *me* any! Haw! Haw!" Gamal continued laughing. "Haw! Haw!"

"They were rude, weren't they!" Adahy laughed with the camel. "But you probably wouldn't have liked it anyway, so no real loss there."

"Yesss, I suppose you're right," Gamal sighed.

"Why not?" Dustu asked. "What does wine taste like?"

"It's bitter," said a little bird that landed on Gamal's rump. "Oh, sorry, I didn't mean to eavesdrop on your conversation."

"We don't mind if you listen in," Adahy told the little bird. "So how do you know what wine tastes like?"

"Well," the little bird chirped, "I was thirsty so I took a sip from a cup—when the human didn't see—and I thought it was nasty. But even worse, after that when I tried to fly, it made me fly in circles and then I crashed into a tree!"

"Oh, no," the fairies sympathized. "Were you OK after that?"

"Yes, I was," he chirped back. "Did I hear you talking about the amazing human that does miracles? The man Jesus?"

"Yes," Gamal answered. "Have you heard of Him?"

"Most certainly, many of us birds know of Him. Did you know that He can heal people?" he asked.

"We have heard, but please tell us what you know," Awinita asked.

"OK," the little bird agreed. "What I saw was a man whose boy was very sick—nearly dead. The man went to Jesus and asked if He would come and cure his son. Jesus just told him that his son was healed. Instead of being angry that Jesus wouldn't come with him, he believed what Jesus had said. I was curious so I followed the man. When we were on the way to his house, some of his servants ran up to him and told him that his son was healed! The man asked when he was healed, and they told him. It was the exact time that Jesus had said that his son was healed! So, Jesus can heal from a long way away! He doesn't even have to be there!"

"That's wonderful!" Dustu said excitedly. This was great news for Dustu, because Waya was far away. Jesus could bring him back to life even from Jerusalem!

Chapter 24

Oasis

After a long day of traveling, everyone—fairy, human, and animal—was happy to stop at an oasis—a place that had water in an otherwise dry land. This place, with a plentiful water well, was surrounded by many palm trees. There were even some vendors of food and supplies selling their wares in the shade of the tall trees.

The people gave water and grain to their animals, then they let them graze on the green grass growing around the oasis. Others made fires in the fire-pits to cook their food. The fairies sat up in a palm tree and ate their dinner. Then they watched as some of the people set up tents for the evening, and some who just unrolled blankets onto the ground. Tomorrow would be another long day, and many wanted to get some rest.

But, there were some who did not want to rest. They gathered in the area where the vendors had their tents and shops. As the evening wore on, the people there became louder and louder with their talking and laughing.

Dustu was curious. Awinita and Adahy had settled down on Gamal's packs next to a palm tree. With a quick glance at them, Dustu crept away. While invisible, he flew over to perch on a vendor's tent roof. He had a great view of the loud men below as they sat around the fire and drank from bottles of wine. The more they drank, the louder they became. Some of them stood up and then fell back down again. They were drunk!

Dustu watched as the wine made them act silly. One fat man tried to stand up, but fell over onto his back and his feet flew up into the air! The man laughed as he tried to stand again. This time he fell sideways into his dinner. Dustu saw that he had knocked his wine bottle over, spilling some onto a plate.

Dustu wanted to taste this wine stuff that made the men silly, so he knew this was his chance. He quietly fluttered his wings and lightly flew down to the ground. The firelight danced across the laughing men, but Dustu didn't think they would notice him. Even though invisible, he still cast a shadow.

He carefully crept to the plate and looked at the red liquid spilled across it. He touched it with his finger and then put his finger in his mouth to taste it ... *YUK!* he thought as he grimaced and then he dry-heaved once. *This stuff is nastier than the seaweed!* He loudly spit the wine out of his mouth.

Even in their drunken state, several men heard Dustu spit. "Did you hear that?" one exclaimed.

"Yeah!" another shouted in alarm. "Snake!"

"Snake?" another yelled out, "Where?"

"Here!" the first man pointed in Dustu's direction. "I heard it hiss here!"

Even though the men were drunk, they weren't too drunk to begin beating the area with blankets! Dustu backed up and barely avoided getting smacked with the flailing cloths as the men ferociously tried to scare the "snake" away. Again and again they whipped the ground with their blankets. Dustu jumped frantically from one spot to another, barely avoiding being hit. Then one of the men kicked the things on the ground where Dustu had tasted the wine. The bags and dishes flew out! A plate barely missed Dustu's head as he quickly scrambled to fly away.

The ruckus woke Awinita and Adahy. "Where's Dustu?" they both questioned at the same time. Just then, Dustu appeared and nearly crash-landed next to them.

"Where were you?" Awinita asked with her fists on her hips. "You're supposed to be asleep!"

"Well," he stammered, "I heard those men over there having such a good time, and I was curious, and they had wine, and I wondered what it tasted like, so I took a taste when they weren't looking, and I thought it was nasty, and then I almost puked, so I spit it out, and they thought I was a snake, and they tried to beat me with blankets, and ..."

"What?"

"... and then I flew back here."

"Boy," Adahy shook his head, "if there is trouble anywhere, you will surely find it!"

"I didn't mean any harm," Dustu said quietly. "I was just curious."

"Dustu," Awinita sighed. "You need to be more careful. These humans are so much larger that we are, and they could seriously hurt you without meaning to. Do you understand me? You need to keep your distance from them."

Dustu shrugged, "Yes, I guess so. But how can they drink that stuff ... that wine stuff. It's terrible!"

"I think they like it because it dulls their senses and helps them forget their worries and problems, but they don't think about how those same worries and problems are still there. Sometimes when they wake up, they find that getting drunk only made things worse."

"So, at that wedding, did Jesus make nasty wine that makes people drunk?" Dustu asked.

"I don't know for sure, but I doubt it. He probably made a nice tasting wine that made the people happy, but not drunk. I'm sure His wine was special."

Chapter 25

Sheep and Goats

The next morning the caravan was on its way again. The sun beat down upon them as they traveled. About noon, the caravan stopped for a short while so that the animals could be given water and the people could eat lunch.

A man approached the leader of the caravan and asked if he could join them for a brief time. He needed to get his sheep and goats to the next town, and it was much safer to travel with a caravan rather than alone … because there were robbers in the area. The caravan leader agreed, and the man herded his small group of sheep and goats along with the caravan as it began to move onward.

After a couple of hours travel, the fairies could hear the sheep complaining.

"I'm tired!"

"My hooves hurt!"

"I'm hot! It's so hot!"

An annoyed goat blurted out, "That's because you're covered in wool!"

Another goat interrupted, "Well, *I'm* not covered in wool and I'm hot too!" And then he continued, "And I'm sick and tired of all these flies!"

Another sheep said, "I'm hungry; I want to graze … but where can we graze on this dusty road?"

Dustu thought-called out to them, "The caravan will probably stop tonight at an oasis where there is good grass, so just be patient."

Awinita and Adahy just looked at each other, each thinking *Dustu is talking about being patient?* And then they smiled, shaking their heads.

"Aren't you a fairy?" an ill-tempered sheep asked, "What do *you* know about grazing?"

"I know that grazing is about green grass, and there was plenty at the oasis we stopped at last night."

"The fairy-kid is right," said an old goat. "But I know about the very best grazing ever! It was almost like a miracle."

"Tell us!" the hungry sheep eagerly demanded.

"Well," the old goat began, "I was with another herd before our master bought me and we were on a grassy hill, grazing, but the grass was just so-so. While we were eating, we saw a Man coming to it and He was surrounded by herds and herds of humans. When He got to the top of the hill, He sat down to talk to them. As soon as He sat, the grass became sweet and wonderful. While He talked, we grazed and stuffed ourselves. The grass was so wonderful—like it was magically delicious."

"What did the Man tell the human herd?" the sheep asked.

"He said a lot of things. He told them that they are blessed if they are good and kind to each other, and to resist evil, and for them to not seek revenge, and for them to treat their enemies with kindness, and not to swear, and … I wish I could remember it all. He told them lots of things, and they all listened."

"Sounds like good advice. Who was this Man?" the sheep asked.

"I think He was called 'Jesus, the Teacher,'" The old goat replied.

"We've heard of Him!" Dustu interrupted. "We're going to find Him!"

"Good idea," the old goat nodded. "And if you do find Him, please thank Him for me for the fantastic grass."

"Sure," Dustu smiled, "I'll try to remember to do that."

Chapter 26

Mouse Stories

As they approached the next oasis, the sun was setting. The man with the sheep and goats left for the nearby town. The caravan set up camp again, and everyone relaxed and ate dinner around the campfires.

The man who had bought bags and bags of grain (before their journey started) was offering it for sale to the people of the caravan. As he unloaded and sold the grain, he often spilled some onto the remaining bags in his cart. The fairies quickly gathered some of the spilled grain.

A mouse sat on the edge of the cart and watched them. "Hey, fairies, leave some for me!" the mouse thought-called to them.

"Who said that?" Adahy thought-called back.

"Me! Over here! On the back of the cart."

In the dim light, Adahy looked over toward the voice. There he saw a fat mouse. "Hello there. Don't worry, there is plenty of spilled grain here for all of us."

"Oh, it's not just for me," the mouse explained. "It's for my family." Suddenly, about twelve little mice popped up onto the cart.

Adahy laughed, "Well, that's a nice family you have there, and I still think there's plenty here for everyone."

Adahy, Awinita, and Dustu finished filling their bags and then they flew over to the back of the cart. They waited for the mouse and his many children to gather grain into their cheeks. Then the mice joined them. "Where do you live?" Adahy asked.

With bulging cheeks packed tightly with grain, the plump mouse thought to Adahy, "Over there." He pointed toward a rickety old wooden shack away from all the oasis activity. He motioned for the fairies to follow as he ran toward it—with his family scurrying quickly behind him.

The mice arrived at the shack and slipped into it through a split in the wood siding. The crack was big enough for the fairies to enter as well. Inside, with only moonlight shining through the windows, they saw many, many more mice!

"We tend to have large families," the mouse explained after he removed the grain from his cheeks.

"Yes, we can see that," Adahy laughed as he smiled at all the mice who were staring wide-eyed at them.

The mouse said to the others, "Next group can go, but be careful that the humans don't see you. There's plenty of grain for us all."

As the next group left, Adahy introduced himself and the others, "Hello, I'm Adahy and this is Awinita and this is Dustu."

"It's nice to meet you," the mouse smiled. "I am Mike, and this is my family. We live here because my family is smaller now."

"Smaller?" Dustu asked incredulously. "There are *more* of you?"

"Don't be rude!" Awinita scolded him.

"It's fine," said Mike, "but yes, my family is quite large. As they grow up and start their own families, some leave with the many caravans that stop here. They want to 'see the world,'" he said as he rolled his eyes. "They don't know that it doesn't change much, at least around this country. Mostly heat and dust, you know."

"It's a lot different from where we come from," Awinita said. "We are from across the great sea. We are on a journey to find Jesus of Nazareth, the Savior of the world."

"My, my!" Mike said in awe. "You *have* come a great distance. Yes, we have heard of Jesus, the Nazarene. I have heard many miraculous stories about Him."

"Tell us, Papa!" one of the small mice children called out.

"Did I tell you how Jesus heals sick people?"

The little mouse shook his head so hard that his big ears flipped about.

"I heard from a very honest source, my fourth cousin that is, that He healed a leper—several of them, actually."

"Do you mean a 'leopard'? A big cat?" A little mouse asked.

"No, not a 'leopard,' a 'leper,'" Mike corrected.

"Sir, what's a 'leper'?" Dustu asked.

"Oh, it's a human with an awful sickness that makes their skin all thick and lumpy. It's a very terrible thing."

"Yes," the other mice quickly nodded their heads in agreement. "Very terrible."

"Lepers are also called 'unclean' and other humans can sometimes get it if they come too close and touch them."

"Can animals get it? Like mice?" a young mouse asked nervously.

"Can fairies get it?" Dustu asked in alarm.

"I don't think so," Mike continued. "People are very cruel to lepers. They call them ugly names and run from them. Sometimes they throw rocks at them to make them leave—just like they throw stuff at us to make us run away. Very terrible. I feel sorry for them."

"So, please tell us what happened—about Jesus, I mean," Awinita asked.

"Well, Jesus was going to a city—I forget which one—and a leper ran up to Him and bowed down low to Him and said, 'Lord, if you wish, You can make me clean!'

"Jesus felt sorry for him and reached out and touched him, saying, 'I will; be clean.' Instantly the man was clean! He had no more leprosy. It was all gone!"

"Wow!" all the mice squeaked.

"And, I heard from my thirteenth cousin that Jesus also healed ten lepers, all at once."

Dustu leaned over toward Adahy and whispered, "Did he just say his 'thirteenth' cousin?"

Adahy grinned and nodded.

"But ... you know what?" Mike continued.

"No," the young mice answered impatiently. "What?"

"Only one leper came back and thanked Jesus," Mike finished the story.

"My goodness!" Awinita gasped. "Only one? Really?"

"Yes," he shook his head with disgust.

"I can't believe how incredibly rude they were," she said with amazement.

*

When all the mice had returned from gathering grain, they all ate together, including the fairies. After dinner, the young mice wanted to hear more of the miracles of Jesus. The adult mice told the stories that they had heard from other mice traveling with the many caravans that had passed by.

"I heard that Jesus can and has healed the blind," an older mouse named Uncle Bernie began. "As He walked by, blind beggars would call out to Him, saying 'Have mercy on us!' and He would heal their blindness and then they could see!"

"Wow," said three mice who were sitting close together. "How awful to be blind!"

"And, there was this one blind man who was born that way. Jesus made a little bit of mud and put it on the man's eyes and told him to wash it off in the pool of Siloam. The blind man was led there and as soon as he had washed the mud off, he could see! The people who knew him saw that he was now healed and they were amazed. They took him to the religious leaders—the priests. They didn't believe that the man had really been blind—they figured that it was some sort of trick—so they called his parents. The parents told them that yes, he had been born blind. Instead of being happy about it, do you know what the priests said?"

"No! Tell us!"

"They said that the Person who healed the blind man was not of God because He healed the blind man on the Sabbath, which is a religious day of rest. They simply ignored the wondrous miracle and told the no-longer-blind man to get out!"

"I can't believe it!" Adahy said.

"And they called the man 'blind' … *they* were truly the 'blind' ones," Awinita murmured as she shook her head.

Another mouse spoke up. "I heard that Jesus also healed those with demons!"

"Demons!" the young mice cried out with fear.

"What are 'demons'?" Dustu asked.

"They are evil spirits that can haunt humans," answered Aunt Bertha, a very plump mouse. "There was this one man who had a demon—an unclean spirit, they called it—in him. Jesus was teaching at the synagogue, the church, and the demon yelled out at Jesus. It knew who He was because it called Him 'The Holy One of God.' It yelled for Him to leave it alone! Jesus told the demon to shut up and come out of the man. It screamed horribly and then came out! The people there were stunned and amazed that Jesus had command even over the demons."

The mice and the fairies listened intently.

"And, He made the deaf hear," added Mike. "I heard from my father that He put His fingers into a deaf man's ears, and then He looked up to heaven and said, 'Be opened' and then the person was no longer deaf! He could hear! It was like that everywhere He went. He healed all the sick and broken people, and they all knew He was the One."

"If all these stories we have heard are true, then Jesus must be the Son of God," Awinita said in wonder. Everyone nodded their heads in agreement.

It was getting late, so the fairies left after thanking the mice for a nice evening. They flew over to the camel's packs that were leaning against a tree, and then they quickly fell asleep.

Chapter 27

Robbers!

The caravan was again on its way. The fairies rode on their friend Gamal, the camel. He told them that they would be coming to Jerusalem soon, maybe the day after next. Everyone was happy about that.

The day wore on, and the fairies sometimes dozed off. Gamal's swaying gait seemed to rock them to sleep. Evening was approaching, but they still had some distance to go before reaching the next oasis. The sun had set and it was now dusk. As it got darker, the animals became agitated.

"What's wrong, Gamal?" Adahy asked.

"I'm not sure," he said nervously as he sniffed the air and turned his ears from front to back. "Something's not right."

Adahy, Awinita, and Dustu peered into the darkness in the direction Gamal was indicating. Suddenly, shadows sprang at them! They were men with covered faces!

Robbers!

There was surprise and panic among the caravan. The robbers were there to steal the merchandise the caravan carried. The people screamed as the robbers ran forward to attack! The caravan travelers drew their weapons of swords and spears to fight the robbers.

The fairies quickly made themselves invisible. "We have to help!" Adahy exclaimed as he fluttered his wings and rose up. "Awinita, you stay here! Dustu, you come with me! Stay invisible!"

Adahy and Dustu flew over to the side of the road and picked up small rocks. They then flew behind the robbers and threw the rocks as hard as they could at their heads. The robbers didn't know what was happening as the rocks bounced off the back of their heads. Alarmed, they spun around with their swords drawn, ready to swing—but they saw no one. Who was throwing the rocks? Where were the rocks coming from? Ghosts? They whipped around in confusion as the rocks seemed to fly at them from out of the air! Adahy and Dustu quickly gathered more rocks and continued to pelt the panicked robbers.

Still invisible, Dustu saw some partially dried-up camel and donkey poop. He grabbed some with his bare hands and flew up to the face of one of the robbers. He yanked down the robber's face cover and smeared the poop right into the startled man's face! The man screamed out in terror and staggered backward.

Grinning, Dustu gathered more poop and flew to another robber. The man was yelling as he ran toward the caravan defenders. Dustu flew backwards in front of the robber and jerked down his face cover. Since the robber was yelling, Dustu shoved the poop right into his open mouth! The shocked man staggered, stumbled, and bent over. Then he gagged and spit, and finally he heaved and puked.

Dustu was having fun! He flew up to another robber as the man raised his sharp sword high into the air, ready to strike a caravan traveler who had no weapon. Dustu suddenly became visible in front of the man's face and yelled, "BOO!" and then he instantly became invisible again. The man fell backwards and screamed, "AHHHH! Ghosts!"

Giggling, Dustu flew up to another robber. He made a snarling face and curled up his fingers like claws. He became visible and yelled out, "BAH!" into the startled robber's face. The man shrieked, fell back, and crashed down to the ground. Then he scrambled up and ran away screaming in terror, "Demons! Demons!"

Now Dustu was laughing out loud. He went up to another robber and hollered into his ear, "STOP!" The man jumped and spun around. Seeing no one, he shrieked and ran, screaming, "Ghost! Ghosts!"

Adahy, seeing what Dustu was doing, did the same. He would fly up to a robber and yell in his ear, "BAH!" Each man would swing around, and finding no one there, would run away in fear. Soon all the robbers were gone.

Adahy and Dustu, both laughing, flew back to Awinita. "Did you see that? We scared them off!"

She was laughing too, "Yes, that was great. Did anyone get hurt? Any of the people in the caravan?"

"I don't know; I'll go check," Adahy said as he rose up. Dustu joined him and they flew down the caravan line to see.

They flew by each caravan member and saw no injuries. But the people were greatly confused. "What happened? Why did the robbers just run away? Why were they screaming?" No one knew what had happened, but all the animals knew. They knew that there were fairies traveling with them, and they watched the whole thing. Adahy and Dustu were heroes, and all the animals called out their thanks to them as they flew back to Awinita.

"Dustu, I am so very proud of you," Awinita said, smiling. "Scaring the robbers was great thinking ... and using poop ... well, that was just brilliant ... but you MUST wash your hands thoroughly when we get to the oasis!"

Chapter 28

Unkind Soldier

The caravan stopped at the next oasis. It was totally dark by then and the stars shone brightly above. Another caravan was there as well, but this one had just left Jerusalem and was traveling toward the coast. The caravan leaders talked together about the attempted robbery and the strange mystery of the thieves simply running away. The outgoing caravan leader was grateful for the warning, because it was quite likely that the robbers might try to attack them.

The next morning was bright. Everyone was excited because they would certainly arrive at Jerusalem by the end of the day. There was also excitement within the other caravan, but it was not a happy excitement. A merchant of fine cloth had given a piece of beautiful blue fabric to his daughter, but the girl was not happy.

"I said I wanted purple fabric!" she demanded of her father. "I don't want any more blue! I want purple! I want purple!" she wailed in her tantrum.

"But, my darling, purple is reserved for royalty," her father tried to reason with her. "We don't want to presume ..."

"I don't care! *I* should be treated like royalty! All rich people should! *I want purple!*" she demanded as she threw the blue fabric to the ground, and then stomped off to their tent.

"What a spoiled brat," some nearby people murmured between themselves.

The caravan packed up and was ready to move out. The blue fabric remained on the ground, forgotten. Awinita sat on a branch above and stared down at it. Her own dress of woven vines and grass was tattered and coming apart. She often tried to repair it, but was not very successful. She would eventually need to find new grasses and vines to weave herself a new dress.

Adahy watched the spoiled girl and her father with disdain. Fairy children would never be allowed to act like that. Then he noticed Awinita's interest in the blue cloth that was being trampled into the dirt by camel feet.

The cloth merchant and his servants had taken down their tent and the camels were loaded and ready to go. The caravan moved out and went on their way. The cloth remained behind. No one seemed to care about it, so Adahy became invisible and flew down to it. He picked it up and flew upward, shaking the dirt off it as he landed in the safety of the tree. Awinita watched with surprise as he folded it up and handed it to her.

"The owner of this threw it away, so I thought that you might like it," he smiled at her. "Am I right?"

She eagerly took the cloth from Adahy and gently smoothed the surface of it. "Oh, thank you! It's so beautiful!"

Still smiling, he took a corner of the cloth and held it up to Awinita's shoulder. "This will be beautiful on you, don't you think?"

"Oh," she murmured. "I've never seen a cloth as lovely as this before." She looked back at Adahy and smiled, "Thank you."

*

As their caravan moved out, Awinita got busy. She took the small knife from her sewing bag that was in her pack. She held the cloth up to herself, carefully measuring it against her body, and then she cut it appropriately. She then un-weaved several threads from the cloth's cut edge and ran them through the hole on her tiny thin bone-needle. She worked steadily through the morning.

At noon, the caravan stopped at a small village to give the animals water and to eat lunch. Nearby was a group of Roman soldiers, eating under open tents that were in the shade of many palm trees. The fairies stared at the men. They were big and muscular, and wore uniforms with funny brushy helmets. They looked different from the soldiers on the Roman ship who had captured the sea-man.

One soldier rubbed the back of his hand across his food-smeared mouth and stood up. He walked over to the caravan to speak with the caravan leader. While they were talking, some ragged children ran up and begged for food from the merchants in the caravan. Being kind, several gave the hungry children some food. Then the kids ran to the soldier, and held up their hands and asked for a coin or two. The man angrily swatted his hand at them and growled hatefully for them to scram—go away. The children ran from him with fear.

The fairies watched the mean Roman as he began to walk back to the rest of the soldiers who were still eating under the tents. Suddenly Dustu, invisible, rose up into the air. Before Awinita or Adahy could call him back, he flew over to the unkind soldier. He landed on the ground next to a fallen palm branch. As the man stepped near, Dustu raised the branch and it caught the man's sandaled foot. The man yelled out in surprise as he tripped and fell *splat* onto the ground! The other soldiers saw him fall and began to laugh loudly. The man got himself up, swore, and growled some not-so-nice words to his friends, who were still laughing.

Grinning, Dustu flew back to Awinita and Adahy. "Dustu, why did you do that?" Adahy scolded him.

"You shouldn't try to hurt people, and that man could have been hurt when he fell!" Awinita chastised.

"The Romans are mean! Look how they treated the sea-man and now how that one treated the hungry kids!" Dustu defended himself.

"I know," Awinita sighed, "but do you remember what the old goat told us of Jesus' teachings? About not seeking revenge but instead show kindness to your enemies?"

"Yes, I remember," Dustu answered. "I'm sorry." But then he mumbled under his breath, "but I still think he deserved it."

Then Gamal interrupted, "Not all Romans are cruel. I'll tell you a story that I had heard from one of the other camels. There was a soldier, a Centurion—a higher ranking Roman officer—whose servant was healed by Jesus. What happened was that the Centurion's servant was very sick and dying. The Centurion went to the religious leaders and begged them to find Jesus so that He could heal his servant. They did, and told Jesus that this Roman was not like the others, he was kind to the Jewish people, and even built a synagogue—a church—for them.

"Jesus agreed to travel to the Centurion's home. But, before He arrived there, the Centurion went out to meet Jesus and told Him that he felt unworthy that Jesus should come to his home. He explained that since he was a Roman officer, he gave orders and those orders would be obeyed. He said that he knew that Jesus also only had to say the words and then the servant would be healed.

"Jesus was absolutely amazed at the faith of this Roman soldier! He turned to all those who followed Him and said that He had not seen such faith before, no, not in all of Israel."

*

That afternoon, Adahy and Dustu dozed on and off with the sway of Gamal's stride. It took her all day, but Awinita finally finished her fine new dress. While Adahy and Dustu were napping—and snoring—she quickly undressed from her old and frayed ragged clothing and carefully pulled her new blue dress over her delicate wings.

Adahy and Dustu yawned and stretched as they woke from their naps. They stared at Awinita. With an impish little half-smile, Dustu teased, "Hey, who are you? Where's my sister?"

Awinita pretended to smack him, and he pretended to duck.

Adahy grinned at her and shook his head in wonder, "You look fantastic! I knew that color would look great on you!"

"Thank you, thank you," she mock bowed.

"Hey, let me see!"

With a glance to see if Gamal's master was still napping, Adahy called back to him, "Hold on, Gamal, we'll be right there." Adahy scooped up Awinita and flew out in front of the camel. Awinita smoothed out her skirt to show Gamal the beautiful shimmer of the blue fabric.

"Very nice, little lady, very, very nice," Gamal nodded his head and smacked his thick lips. "Are you also going to make one for the boy?"

Dustu immediately flew up to them and frowned, "No, she is *not*! I'm not wearing a *dress*!"

Then Gamal laughed loudly, "Haw, Haw! Got you, boy! Haw! Haw! Got you I did, indeed!"

Chapter 29

The Vulture

The caravan was passing a graveyard. The happy mood of the travelers quickly turned to sadness, as they watched a grieving family who had just buried a loved one. The family members were crying in sorrow. As the caravan passed, the travelers bowed their heads in respect for the very sad mourners.

There was a big and rather unpleasant looking bird sitting on the dirt roadway ahead. As the caravan approached, the bird stretched its wings and flew over to a tombstone and perched himself there, hunching his bald head down. He saw the fairies staring at him, so he thought-called to them. "Just what do you think you're looking at?"

"Oh, sorry," Adahy apologized. "We didn't mean to stare."

"Well, you are, and it's rude, you know," the ugly bird chastised them.

The fairies flew over to a tree that hung over the cemetery. They settled on a branch so that they could speak with the strange bird.

"We are sorry, sir, it's just that ... we haven't seen any bird like you before," Awinita explained. "Uh, what kind of bird are you, if you don't mind me asking?"

"No, I don't mind. I'm a vulture."

"A vulture," Awinita nodded, "I've never seen any of your kind before."

"Well, there's plenty of us around, but we mostly hang out where there are dead things rotting in the sun."

"Dead things rotting!" Dustu exclaimed. "Why would you want to be around *that*?"

"Because that's what we eat!" the vulture replied gleefully. "Yum!"

"Gross!" Dustu grimaced.

"No, it's what we do."

"So, why are you here ... at this cemetery?" Adahy asked.

"Because it's my favorite place, that's why," the vulture said as he stretched his boney neck out and then hunched down again.

"But the people put their dead in the ground where you can't get to them, right?" Adahy added.

"Yes," the vulture said with disappointment, "they do. And sometimes they put their dead in tombs."

"What's a 'tomb'?" Dustu asked.

"Well," the vulture explained, "it's a small building or a cave. They are used for the highly honored dead or for rich people." The vulture paused and then said happily, "But sometimes they also bring dead animals here and just dump them. That's when we get a feast!"

"Eeewww," Awinita said softly to herself, making a face.

"Not much in the way of good eating here today though," the vulture continued unhappily as he turned his head toward the family burying their loved one.

"You don't eat *people,* do you?" Awinita asked in horror.

140

"Sure," the vulture answered with surprise. "Why not? If they're dead, it's a fine meal."

The fairies stared in horror at the vulture.

"Thankfully there's no chance at all of a dead person coming out of one of these tombs to be your dinner," Adahy said with relief.

"Oh, but you are so wrong!" the vulture exclaimed as he shifted his feet on the tombstone. "There was this one time when I saw a dead man walk right out of a tomb! He was all wrapped up in cloth … that's what the humans do to their dead—they wrap them up."

"No, no way … how can that be?"

"I'll tell you," the vulture began. "I was at a cemetery not far from Jerusalem. A good man named Lazarus had been buried inside in a small cave and they put a large stone in front of it. The family and their friends cried and cried, because they loved this man so. They had sent word to a Man, named Jesus, who was a good friend of theirs."

"Yes," Dustu blurted out. "We know of Him!"

"As I was saying, before I was so rudely interrupted," the vulture looked sideways at Dustu and then continued, "this Jesus came and told the people to move aside the stone that covered the cave entrance. The sister of Lazarus said that he had been dead for four days and he would stink!" The vulture paused his story and said wistfully, "Ah, my favorite smell … the smell of rotting flesh." Then he continued, "Jesus looked up to heaven and said 'Father, I thank You for hearing Me. I say this so that the people here will believe that You have sent Me!' Then Jesus said with a loud voice, 'Lazarus! Come out!'

"To the amazement of everyone there, Lazarus walked out of the cave!" The vulture gave a guilty little laugh and admitted, "I was so shocked that I nearly fell off the tombstone I was sitting on!" Then he continued his story, "Lazarus was still bound up in the grave wrappings, so Jesus told the people to unwrap him. He was indeed alive! Jesus had raised him from four days of death! It was incredible … just incredible." The vulture shook is bald head, remembering the amazing event.

Dustu listened and marveled at the story. His hopes for Jesus bringing Waya back from death were confirmed. He couldn't wait to find Him!

Chapter 30

Olive Grove

They had arrived! At the outskirts of Jerusalem within a grove of olive trees, the caravan rested from their long journey. The evening was getting darker so the merchants said their good-byes to one another and wished everyone good fortunes. One by one they left, and then it was time for Gamal's master to go. The fairies thanked Gamal for the ride and hoped that they would see their friend again in the future. Then they gathered their belongings and flew into the orchard. They found several olive trees that grew close together so they tucked their bags between them. It had gotten very dark by then, so they sat there and ate their dinner.

"We need to replenish our food supplies," Awinita said as she lifted two nearly-empty bags to show Adahy.

"Yes," Adahy agreed. "We'll see what we can do about that tomorrow." Then Adahy shook his shoulders nervously. "I feel like … we're being watched," he said as he looked about.

"Now that you mention it, so do I," Awinita agreed. They both looked around, searching the darkness. Seeing nothing unusual, they rolled out their mats and stretched out under the olive tree. Soon they were fast asleep.

*

The next morning, they awoke to the sounds of whispers, "Look how handsome he is!"

"Oh, I agree, very good-looking ... and strong! Look at those muscles!"

"And his wings! Look how big they are!"

"Do you think he's married?"

"I don't know ... there's a girl there ... but it looks like she has a broken wing."

Adahy, Awinita, and Dustu instantly sat up. There in front of them were three fairies! All young pretty teenage girls!

Dustu blurted out, "Who are you?" Then he rubbed his eyes.

Now wide awake, Adahy stood up and greeted them, "Hello. My name is Adahy, and this is Awinita and Dustu. Do you live here?"

The girls giggled, and one of them replied, "Yes, we do. This orchard is our home."

"I see," Adahy smiled at them. "I hope you didn't mind that we spent the night here."

"No, we don't mind at all," the oldest-looking girl answered as she looked Adahy up and down. "*You* can stay as long as you like."

"Ummm," one girl said shyly, "I've never heard of a name like 'Adahy' before ... what does it mean?"

"It means 'woodsman,'" he answered, smiling. "And 'Awinita' means 'fawn,' and 'Dustu' means 'little tree frog.'"

The girls grinned at Dustu, finding his name amusing. "That's very interesting," the oldest girl smiled.

"We had a friend named 'Waya' which means 'wolf,' but he died in the great sea," Dustu interrupted. "We're going to find Jesus of Nazareth and I'm going to ask Him to bring Waya back alive to us."

"Oh!" the girls exclaimed. "We have heard of Jesus! He has been here in Jerusalem before. He's a great Teacher and He heals the sick and does all kinds of wonderful miracles! And you are in luck, because He is here now! He arrived yesterday for the Passover holiday."

"Yes, they say He is the Son of God!" the other girl eagerly added.

"But some of the temple priests don't like Him, because the people listen to Him instead of them. He teaches with the authority of God. I think they're jealous of Him and the love the people have for Him."

"Thank you for the information," Adahy smiled, nodding to them.

"Would you like to join us for breakfast?" Awinita offered kindly. "We don't have much left, but you are welcome to join us."

"Thank you, but we have already eaten," the oldest girl replied, not looking at Awinita but instead still staring at Adahy. "Are you planning to stay long?"

"It depends," Adahy answered. "We have come to hear the teachings of the Savior, Jesus, and then return to our people and tell them all we have learned."

"Are you married?" the youngest girl blurted out.

Adahy turned to her, smiling, "No, not yet."

"Do you want to be?" the oldest girl asked boldly.

Adahy laughed, "One day, yes, I want to be." He gave a quick glance at Awinita, but she didn't notice.

"You could find a wife here and stay in our land. It's very nice living here," she added hopefully.

The girls continued to flirt with Adahy. Dustu ate his food, paying no attention. But Awinita watched as the girls couldn't take their eyes off Adahy. Of course they couldn't, he was very handsome and strong. But far more important than that was the fact that he was a good man. A wonderfully kind man. The best *unmarried* man any girl could ask for. She couldn't blame the girls as they ogled him, but still she couldn't help feeling the sting of jealously ... even a bit of anger. He was HER friend ... her BEST friend.

*

The fairy girls told Adahy that they had seen a donkey cart parked at the edge of the olive tree grove and that it was going into Jerusalem later that morning. The fairies thanked the girls for the information, said good-bye, and then flew over to the cart. While Adahy carried Awinita, Dustu easily managed to carry all their bags because they were mostly empty now.

The donkey who was hitched to the small cart was muttering to himself when Adahy flew up to him. "Hi! We are going to Jerusalem and we need a ride. Can you help us?"

The donkey's head jerked back in surprise, and then he said, "Sure, fairy person, hop on. We'll be leaving soon. My master is ... oh, here he comes now."

A heavy-set man walked up to the donkey. He took the long lead rope and started off down the path toward one of Jerusalem's gates, pulling on the rope, "Come on, Chamor, let's get going."

The fairies, invisible, sat on the front of the cart. The cart jerked up and down as the wheels rolled across the very bumpy dirt path. "My name is Adddahy," Adahy tried to talk as the cart wheel hit a hole. "And this is Awinita, and this is Dustuuuu," his voice stuttered again as the cart wheel dipped into another hole.

"This is a rough path, but the road is just ahead. It's a much smoother ride on it, so just hold on a little more. We're almost there," the donkey thought back. "My name is Chamor. My master and I are partners. We haul things for people who pay us. I'm very good at my job. Did I mention that my master and I are partners? Well, we are … but sometimes he forgets about me. Like now, before we left. I sure am thirsty. I wish I could talk to humans, I wish I could tell my master to not forget to give me water! After all, we're partners, you know."

"Yes, that's …" Adahy started to thought-speak but Chamor interrupted.

"I'll bet you didn't know that long ago, there was a lady-donkey who did actually talk! Yes, it's true. She talked to her master with people words and he understood her. It was a very long time ago, but I'll tell you the story. A man named Balaam saddled his she-donkey and started on a journey to visit a rich king. During the journey, the donkey saw a mighty Angel of the Lord standing in the way, and he had his sharp sword drawn! Of course, she was frightened, so she turned toward a field instead of going forward. Her master, Balaam, smacked her with his whip to make her go the right way.

"Then the Angel of the Lord stood in her way again, between two walls in a vineyard. The lady-donkey tried to turn away and accidentally squashed Balaam's foot against the wall. He smacked her again with his whip, trying to make her go forward.

"A bit farther ahead, between two tight spaces where the lady-donkey could not turn right or left because it was so narrow, the Angel *again* stood blocking her way. So, the lady-donkey had no choice but to fall down. Balaam was so mad that he hit her with a heavier stick!"

147

"Oh!" Awinita exclaimed. "Hitting her was cruel!"

"Yes, it was," Chamor nodded his head. "My master is not cruel. He never hits me. We're partners, and partners don't hurt each other."

Chamor shook a fly off his ear and continued with his story. "Then, a miracle happened. The Lord made the lady-donkey speak! She said to her master, 'What have I done to you that would make you strike me three times?' Balaam said back to her, 'Because you didn't obey me! If I had a sword, I would kill you right now!' And the donkey said to Balaam, 'Don't you know that I am your donkey who has served you since you first owned me? Have I ever disobeyed you until now?' Balaam answered, 'No.'

"Then the Lord made the Angel with his drawn sword turn visible to Balaam. Balaam was shocked! He immediately bowed down flat on the ground. Then the Angel said to Balaam, 'I have tried to stop you three times, and each time your donkey saw me and tried to go another way. Had she not done this, I would have surely killed you, but I would not have killed her.' So, the donkey saved Balaam's life."

Chamor paused so Dustu quickly thought to him while he had the chance, "But why did the Angel want to kill Balaam?"

"We donkeys think it was because the Lord told Balaam to go to the king, but to only say what the Lord wanted him to say, and nothing more. We suspect that Balaam had other intentions, so that's why the Lord sent the Angel. In the end it worked out OK, because Balaam did go to the king and said only what the Lord wanted him to say."

"I'll bet that Balaam was surprised to hear his donkey talk!" Awinita quickly thought to Chamor.

"I would imagine so …"

"I'll bet your master would be surprised if *you* spoke," Dustu interrupted.

"I can speak; he just can't understand me ... all people are like that, you know ... I sure am thirsty."

"Chamor," Adahy said before the donkey could start again. "How about I fly up to your master and whisper in his ear that you need water?"

"Oh, would you please? That would be great. I'm so thirsty. He doesn't mean to be cruel; he just forgets sometimes that we animals have feelings too, even though we're partners, you know."

So, Adahy flew up to the man. Hovering next to his ear, Adahy whispered ever so softly that Chamor was thirsty. He whispered it over and over. The man brushed at his ear, but didn't seem alarmed at the gentle voice he kept hearing.

By then they had reached the smooth road leading into Jerusalem. Off to the side was a watering trough and the man led Chamor over to it. As Chamor gratefully (and noisily!) slurped up the cool water, the man rubbed him between the ears and murmured to him, "Sorry, old boy. I have a lot on my mind." He continued to rub and pet Chamor. "Drink up, little partner."

Chapter 31

Jerusalem

The donkey cart couldn't go any farther. The street entering Jerusalem was packed with throngs of happy people. They were calling out "Blessings! Blessed is He who comes with the name of the Lord!"

The fairies were very curious, so they flew up to a tree off to the side of the road ahead. As they sat on a branch, they saw people spread their clothes on the street, and they saw them cut branches off low hanging palm trees and place them also on the street. Then they saw a Man, riding on a young donkey that had colorful robes across its back.

The Man was Jesus! They had found Jesus!

The people all continually and joyfully called out, "Blessed be the Kingdom of our Lord! Blessed is the Holy One of God!"

The fairies could feel the excitement of the people, as they too were overcome with joy. The Savior of the World was passing just below them! They were overwhelmed with the unimaginable honor of being in the presence of the Son of God!

After Jesus and the huge crowd passed by, they flew back to Chamor to tell him the good news, but he already knew! "Yes, Jesus is here! I heard my young nephew, Ayir, calling out to all animals, 'Look at me! Riding on me is the Son of the Most High! I am truly blessed to serve the Lord Jesus! Look at me!'"

Soon the number of people cleared out and the donkey cart was able to get onto the street. They passed through the gate into Jerusalem. The fairies had never seen such a place like this before! They marveled at the high walls which surrounded the city. Everywhere colorful flags waved in the breeze. The city was huge!

The streets were crowded with merchants and travelers who were there for the Passover celebrations. The merchants called out to advertise their wares and musicians played their musical instruments. The people were smiling and happy as they went about preparing for the holy celebration of Passover.

The fairies wanted to see where Jesus had gone, but He was nowhere to be seen. In the distance they saw a marvelous building.

"Is that the Temple?" Adahy asked.

"Yes, it is," Chamor answered. "I know that Jesus taught there before."

They guessed that Jesus would probably go there again, so they thanked Chamor for his help and then decided to go to the Temple and wait. They flew up to a decorative ledge which was high above the wide steps that led into the magnificent church. They didn't have long to wait.

The fairies sat up on the narrow ledge with their legs hanging over. Casually swinging their feet back and forth, they watched the people below them come and go. The regular people who came to worship were dressed in modest clothing, but the temple priests were dressed in the very finest robes made of expensive fabric! All the people bowed low to them as they passed.

In the distance, the fairies saw a group coming. Was Jesus among them? They waited anxiously as the group came closer. Yes! He was! Dustu began to get up off the ledge, but Adahy stopped him. "We can't go to Him right now, He's surrounded by too many."

Jesus approached the temple and began to climb the steps. The fairies watched with awe as He passed into the Temple entrance below them. Jesus' followers suddenly stopped when they heard a loud roar from Him, "What is going on in here!"

White birds suddenly flew out from the Temple entrance! They sang out happily, "We're free! We're free!" Then a broken birdcage flew out of the Temple and bounced down the steps. Next there were frightened and angry voices yelling from inside!

The wide-eyed followers of Jesus quickly backed down the steps. What was going on inside? The fairies wondered as they leaned forward. Then a basket of coins flew out of the Temple entrance! The basket bounced down the steps and coins sprayed out everywhere! The coins made tinkling sounds as they bounced and rolled down the steps. Then a merchant ran out of the Temple shrieking! "No! Stop!"

Then a table flew out! It crashed on the steps and bounced down, flying apart more and more each time it crashed against the stone steps. Next a chair flew out!

This was becoming very entertaining!

Another merchant ran out, screaming "Aaaeee!" More coins flew out and bounced clinking down the steps. The two merchants scrambled to collect the money.

"How dare you mock My Father's House!" they heard Jesus yell. "Get out!"

Then another table flew out! It landed on all its legs, flipped over into the air, then bounced down the steps and crashed upside down at the bottom.

"Good one!" Adahy laughed.

More white birds flew out of the Temple entrance. "Thank you my Lord!" they sang as they flew to freedom.

A bag of coins flew out! Then a man ran out and tried to rescue it before it split apart, but he was too late as the money spewed out. The other merchants quickly began to scoop up the new money and put it into their pockets. "No," the other man screamed. "Mine! It's mine!"

Two more chairs flew out! Then a basket! The basket bounced off the side wall and flipped in the air, and landed upside down on one man's head! He didn't even seem to notice as he bent over, greedily collecting the coins.

The fairies were laughing as more furniture flew out of the Temple. Several more men came running out with their hands up, squealing in despair!

Then Jesus appeared in the entrance and angrily called out, "My house is a house of prayer! You have made it a den of thieves!"

The merchants scurried away as some of the followers of Jesus collected the broken things at the bottom of the steps and moved them aside. The fairies heard them exclaiming their outrage that merchants would sell stuff inside the Holy Temple!

Chapter 32

Passover

The fairies flew inside the Temple and sat on a thick wooden beam high above. An old woman came up to Jesus. She was crippled so bad that she walked all bent over, and she couldn't stand up straight. She had been that way for 18 years! The priests watched to see what Jesus would do. So did the fairies. They leaned forward anxiously waiting to see what would happen. They watched as Jesus gently reached out and placed His hands on her.

He said firmly, "Woman, you are free from your infirmity!" Immediately she stood up straight. She was healed!

The fairies stared wide-eyed at the healed woman as she walked away, singing praises to Jesus and God. Awinita took Adahy's hand and exclaimed, "He is truly the Son of God!"

Then a man humbly walked up to Jesus. One of his hands was all shrunken, withered, and useless. Jesus knew the hearts of the jealous priests who were standing there watching Him, so He asked them, "Is it lawful to do good on the holy day of rest, the Sabbath? To save a life? What man would stand by and let one of his sheep fall into a pit and not rescue it, even though it was on the Sabbath, where the law states that no work is to be done on that day? Well?"

None of the priests answered. Then Jesus said to the man with the deformed hand, "Stretch out your hand." The man did, and it was instantly healed!

It was like that all day long. The fairies watched as people entered the temple with their sick and lame, and then joyously left healed and whole!

As the fairies sat on their high perch in the Temple, they were amazed at each healing. Even though they had heard of His miracles from the animals, it was witnessing them happening in front of their eyes that was even more incredible!

Some of the priests wondered, could this amazing Man be the foretold Savior of the World? The Son of God? They knew about the promises in their ancient writings, so they wondered. But most of the priests whispered among themselves, desiring to accuse Jesus of breaking the religious laws because He healed people on the Sabbath. They secretly plotted with each other. They wanted to get rid of Him, because the people wanted Him, not them. They had to find a way to stop Him ... even if they had to kill Him!

The fairies watched the happy events below them. But Adahy noticed the jealous priests whispering among themselves and frowning as they glanced back at Jesus.

"You stay here, I'm going to see what those men are up to," Adahy said as he stood up and then flew toward them.

*

Adahy followed the priests who were looking back at Jesus with hate in their eyes. Invisible, he silently flew alongside and slightly above them, listening, as they whispered among themselves. The priests entered a small room and Adahy followed them in. He flew over to a window and landed on the sill. Adahy's eyes widened in alarm as he listened to them plot against Jesus.

Then a servant came into the room and said that there was a man waiting who could help them. The priests agreed to see the man, and he was brought in. In near disbelief, Adahy listened as the man asked what they would pay if he could deliver Jesus to them—away from the crowds of people who loved and followed Him. They bargained ... and finally agreed on the price of 30 pieces of silver.

When the man left, Adahy quickly slipped out through the door and flew back to Awinita and Dustu. "You won't believe this, but those men are planning to get Jesus!"

"What?" Awinita gasped. "Get Jesus? What do you mean?"

"I think they mean to get rid of Him, maybe even kill Him."

"We can't let that happen!" Dustu exclaimed.

"Absolutely, we can't," Adahy agreed.

"We need to warn Him," Awinita said firmly. "He has healed all the people here, and it looks like He is getting ready to leave. Everyone is talking about the Passover dinner tonight."

"We need to follow Him, and then maybe we can tell Him what's going on."

*

The fairies followed Jesus and twelve men to a house. The group climbed steps up to a large room upstairs and the fairies silently followed. In the room was a long table covered with food! The fairies flew to and sat on a small table on the opposite side of the room.

Jesus and the group of men sat down to eat, and the fairies got a good look at them. Adahy gasped! He could hardly believe his eyes! One of them was the man he had seen with the priests! Adahy whispered to Awinita and Dustu, "See that man there at the end of the table? He is the man who was paid 30 pieces of silver! He is going to betray Jesus!"

"No! How can that be?" Awinita said, confused. "He is one of Jesus' closest followers!"

"We have to warn Him!" Dustu added, horrified.

"We will," both Adahy and Awinita assured him.

The men all began to eat, and during the meal Jesus said, "One of you will betray me."

They were all shocked, even the man at the end of the table, who they heard was named Judas.

"Master, is it I?" they each asked in dismay.

Finally Judas asked, "Is it I?"

Then Jesus said, "As you say."

The fairies were surprised that Jesus already knew of the plot to get Him! But then they realized, He was Jesus. He knew everything. He probably even knew that *they* were there.

After the Passover dinner, Jesus and His Disciples left the house and walked to the peaceful Garden of Gethsemane. The fairies followed. On the way, all the Disciples vowed that even though they might be faced with death, they would *never* betray or deny Him. Especially Peter, he repeated firmly that he would go to prison or die first! But Jesus sadly said to Peter, "Before the rooster crows, you will have denied knowing Me three times." Peter continued to argue that he would *never* do that, but Jesus just sadly shook His head.

They arrived at the beautiful garden, and it was quite dark by then. The fairies wanted to talk to Jesus, but He was never alone. Jesus said to the men, "Sit here and keep watch while I go pray."

Jesus walked a bit farther into the garden. Now was their chance to talk to Him! They flew across the grass toward Jesus but He, full of sorrow, fell to His knees and then to the ground. Because He knows everything, He knew of the terrible things that were going to happen to Him. In agony, He prayed to God, "Father, I wish I did not have to do this, but it is Your will, not Mine, that I obey." He was in such pain in His spirit, that the sweat on His face became big drops of blood!

Shocked, Adahy, Awinita, and Dustu instantly stopped. They stared in horror at Jesus as the drops of blood on His forehead fell to the ground. Then to their amazement, the darkness of night suddenly turned bright. The garden around them glowed with an incredible brilliance, yet it did not hurt their eyes. Within the light an amazing being appeared! An Angel!

In awe, the fairies backed up into the shadows. What were they seeing? Adahy, Awinita, and Dustu stared in wonder as the magnificent Angel comforted Jesus.

After a short while, the fairies watched as Jesus got up off the ground and walked back to His Disciples. They were all sound asleep. He woke Peter and said to him, "Couldn't you stay awake one hour for Me?" Peter apologized and then Jesus went back to pray some more. The fairies waited quietly in the shadows, still staring at the incredible Angel.

A bit later, Jesus rose from His knees and walked back to His men, but they were again all sound asleep. He woke them again. They said they were sorry and couldn't explain why they were so sleepy.

Jesus went back to pray for the third time, and when He was finished, He found them all sound asleep again! He woke them and said, "The time has come. I am betrayed into the hands of sinners."

The magnificent Angel disappeared and the garden became dark again ... but not for long. New lights were appearing in the distance. They were not Angelic lights--these were lights from lanterns and torches from a mob of people. The fairies could hear the rough voices and shouts as the angry mob came closer and closer through the garden. When the mob arrived, the fairies could see that they also had swords and spears!

Adahy scooped up Awinita into his arms and flew to the safety of a branch in an olive tree. Dustu was right behind them.

"What's going on?" Dustu whispered.

"Look!" Awinita said, pointing. "There's Judas! He just went up to Jesus and kissed Him on the cheek." As soon as he had kissed Jesus, the angry people surrounded Him.

Jesus asked, "Who are you looking for?"

They answered, "Jesus of Nazareth."

Then Jesus said, "I am He." As soon as He said it, the mob fell backwards!

"Whoa!" Dustu exclaimed. "Did you see that?"

The surprised people got up off the ground and Jesus asked them again, "Who are you looking for?"

And they answered again, "Jesus of Nazareth."

Jesus said back to them, "Like I told you, here I am, so let My men go." Then He added, "Are you coming after Me with weapons like I am some kind of thief? I sat in the Temple all day, and now you come after Me here?"

The men grabbed at Jesus. Peter, in great anger, pulled his sword and swung it at the nearest man—a servant of the high priest—and cut off his right ear!

Awinita gasped in horror as the bloody ear fell to the ground. Adahy held Awinita tightly in case they had to quickly fly up to a higher branch to escape a sword fight.

Jesus said to Peter, "Put your sword away. This is what has to happen." And then to the surprise to all, Jesus touched the man's ear and it was healed!

The fairies anxiously watched as the mob forced Jesus to go with them. The followers of Jesus were afraid of the mob, so they all ran away. Peter ran too, but then he turned and followed them from a distance. The fairies flew after Jesus, trying to keep up.

Chapter 33

Arrested!

The fairies followed behind the mob, resting occasionally on a tree branch, but never loosing sight of Jesus as the people noisily moved along. The mob took Jesus to the high priest—one who also never believed Jesus to be the One sent by God. As they approached the house, they could see that it was very ornate and spacious. The fairies followed the priest's men as they roughly shoved Jesus inside. They flew over to a side table and Adahy gently set Awinita down upon it. Invisible, they watched to see what was going to happen to Jesus.

Several other priests were there waiting with some "witnesses" they had gathered to prove that Jesus was a blasphemer (one who spoke against God). These "witnesses" lied about Jesus, accusing Him of all kinds of evil things. They talked on but Jesus said nothing.

Dustu whispered into Awinita's ear, "Why doesn't Jesus defend Himself?"

"I don't know, Dustu" Awinita whispered back.

The high priest (who wanted Jesus to admit wrongdoings) demanded that Jesus speak, and so He did. "I have taught in the churches and to the people; I have not kept any secrets. My teachings were for all to hear," He said firmly, looking the High Priest in the eye.

One of the priest's men slapped Jesus in the face. "Don't You dare speak to the high priest like that!"

Jesus was knocked to the side, but He turned back and stood tall. "If I have spoken evil, then prove it, but if I haven't, then why do you hit Me?"

Dustu jumped up but Awinita grabbed his arm. "No, Dustu, you must not interfere!" she whispered anxiously.

The high priest continued to accuse Jesus and insisted that He answer, "Tell us! Do You say that You are Christ, the Son of God?"

Jesus replied, "If I tell you, you won't believe it. And you still won't let Me go. But, you have said it—I am. And in the future, you will see Me sit at the right hand of God."

The high priest's eyes grew wide and he tore at his clothes. "We have heard it out of His own mouth! He dares to say He is the Son of God! This is blasphemy! He needs to be put to death!"

And the other priests agreed that Jesus should be killed!

The fairies were in shock. What is wrong with these people? Jesus did only good, and they want to kill Him for it? Were they so blind in their jealousy that they couldn't see the miracles that He had performed could *only* be the work of God?

*

Peter had followed the angry mob but was not allowed inside the luxurious house, so he waited at the door. The doorkeeper said to him, "Aren't you one of His friends? Friends of the Man who was just brought in to the high priest?"

"No, you are mistaken," Peter answered, shaking his head.

So Peter left the doorway and went outside. There was a chill in the air, so he walked over to warm himself by the fire pit in the courtyard. While he warmed his hands around the fire, one of the high priest's servants said, "Hey, you *are* one of the followers of that Jesus guy!"

Peter swore and then said, "No, I'm not. I'm just here to get warm."

Then another servant came up and said, "Yes, you are! You are one of His followers!"

Afraid, Peter cursed and swore, "I am not! I don't even know the Man!"

Immediately, a nearby rooster crowed. In shock, Peter remembered what Jesus had said to him: *Before the rooster crows, you will have denied Me three times.* In anguish for his cowardly actions and betrayal, Peter ran away and wept bitterly.

*

The priests ordered that Jesus be delivered to the Roman Governor, Pontius Pilot, for punishment. Horses were brought for the priests to ride on, so Awinita and Adahy sat together on one horse's rump and Dustu sat on another. Everyone else walked toward the Governor's palace.

As the group traveled, the men mocked Jesus. They blindfolded Him and then hit Him in the face. They sneered, "If You're such a great prophet, then tell us who just hit You?" They laughed at Him, hit Him, and even spat in His face. Knowing there was nothing they could do, Adahy and Dustu watched angrily, while Awinita cried softly.

When they arrived at the Governor's palace, it was early morning. The fairies flew to a ledge where they had a clear view of Jesus, the governor's porch, and the mob of accusing priests.

The large group entered the courtyard of the palace and waited for the Governor to appear on the spacious porch. When he did, they wasted no time in accusing Jesus.

"This Man is a criminal! He is a blasphemer!"

Then Governor Pilot answered, "So, take Him and judge Him according to your law."

The priests said, "We cannot put any man to death. You can." Then, because Israel was under Roman rule, the priests accused Jesus of saying that He was the king.

Pilot asked Jesus, "Are You the king of the Jews?"

Jesus answered, "Are you wondering this for yourself or did you hear this about Me?"

Pilot replied, "How would I know; am I a Jew? No, Your own people and their chief priests have brought You here. So, what did You do? Are You their king?"

Jesus explained to Pilot, "My kingdom is not of this world. If it were, then My followers would fight and I would have not been delivered here. But to this end I was born, and for this I came into the world so I can bear witness to truth. Those who hear My truth, know it to be so."

"Truth," Pilot murmured, as he turned back to the crowd. "What is truth?" Then he said loudly to the mob. "I find no fault in this Man!"

The priests immediately came forward and accused Jesus of everything else they could come up with. But Jesus said nothing in return. Pilot asked, "Don't You hear all the things they have accused You of? Don't You want to defend Yourself?"

Jesus didn't answer, so Pilot turned to the priests and said, "I still don't see any wrong-doing in the Man."

The priests yelled out, "He stirs up the people, all the way from Galilee to here!"

Pilot was surprised, "Galilee? Then He is under Herod's rule. He needs to be the one to judge this Man."

The priests grumbled as Pilot directed his men to take Jesus to Herod, who was visiting in Jerusalem for the Passover.

"What's going on?" Dustu asked. "Are they sending Jesus to this 'Herod' guy?"

"It appears so," Adahy replied.

As the group left, the fairies again rode on the horse rumps. Again, the large group traveled across Jerusalem to Herod. Herod was delighted to hear that Jesus was being sent to him. He had heard of all the miracles and very much wanted to meet Him and maybe get a demonstration of His "magic."

When they arrived at Herod's grand house, the fairies flew inside and perched upon a table near the wall. They watched as Herod slowly walked in and then sat in a throne-like grand chair. He was dressed in magnificent brightly colored robes. The fairies had never seen anyone like him before.

Jesus knew Herod had an evil heart, so when Herod asked questions, Jesus didn't answer. The priests who went with Jesus accused Him more and more viciously, hoping that Herod would punish (kill) Him. Since Jesus would not talk or perform any "magic tricks" for him, Herod and his soldiers sneered and mocked Jesus.

Adahy looked over at Dustu. He could see the boy's pointed ears twitching in anger as Herod and his men laughed at and insulted Jesus. He touched Dustu's arm and when Dustu turned to look back, he shook his head "no." He was also outraged at the treatment of Jesus, but he knew they shouldn't interfere.

Even with his cruel heart, Herod also found no fault in Jesus that was worthy of death, so he sent them all back to Pilot. Again, the group returned to the Governor's palace. On the way, Dustu grumbled, "That Herod was a real jerk. I wish I had some of that camel poop to shove into his mouth."

By now, the other priests had called many people to assemble in the courtyard of the Governor's palace. They wanted more public support in their efforts to get rid of Jesus.

The fairies returned to their perch on the ledge. The impatient crowd waited in front of the grand porch for Governor Pilot to appear. When he did, he was annoyed. The priests insisted that he, as governor, punish Jesus. But Pilot said, "I told you that I find no fault in this Man. Even Herod did not find any reason to punish Him."

"He is guilty! He has blasphemed!" the angry priests yelled out.

Then most all the people gathered shouted out, "Punish Him! Crucify Him!"

As the crowd yelled louder and louder, Awinita covered her delicate ears with her hands.

"Look," Pilot said as he tried to quiet the vicious crowd. "I'll have Him whipped and then bring Him back to you." Then Pilot walked off the palace porch.

The mob angrily spoke with one another. The dishonest priests encouraged their anger by telling them that Jesus was dangerous, and an awful sinner, because He pretended to do miracles to fool the people into believing that He was some sort of God. They fueled the mob's viciousness by saying that Jesus did tricks because He was actually partners with the devil!

As Jesus was dragged away by Pilot's soldiers, the fairies followed. The men took Jesus to an area out back of the palace and then they began to mock Him. They stripped Him of His clothes, and then put a purple robe on Him. They handed Him a stick and then they bowed low to Him and sneered, "Hail to the King of the Jews!" Then they laughed and laughed. "Hail to the King!" they continued to mock.

"A king needs a crown!" one soldier laughed, as he went to a thorn bush and cut some small branches off. He carefully wrapped them together into a ring, and walked back, saying with a smirk, "And here is His crown!" He put it onto Jesus' head and pushed it down. The sharp thorns bit into Jesus' scalp, and the blood ran down His face.

The fairies sat on the edge of a cart that was parked nearby. They gasped in horror at the sight, but they could do nothing! Awinita held her hand over her mouth, afraid that she might cry out. Adahy gritted his teeth as he held onto Dustu. The boy wanted to do something … anything! They all did, but they couldn't.

Next the soldiers took the purple robe off Jesus, leaving Him almost naked. Then they hit His body with sticks and hit His face with their fists. When He fell they kicked Him and they spat on Him.

"Why does He let them do this?" Awinita whispered tearfully. "He is the Son of God!"

"Yeah!" Dustu agreed. "Why doesn't He just turn them into cockroaches and stomp their guts out!"

"I don't know. I just don't know," Adahy shook his head sorrowfully.

Then the soldiers dragged Jesus to a post and tied His hands to it. One soldier took a whip and swung it a Jesus! The end of the whip cut into Jesus and the blood poured out, running down His back. Jesus cried out in pain—He couldn't help but cry out as the soldier cruelly struck again and again.

Jesus slumped down, limp. Only His tied hands held Him up against the post. "Don't kill Him," an officer warned. "We have to take Him back to the Governor."

The soldiers jerked Jesus up off the ground. "Get up, King!" they growled. They put the purple robe back on Him, and then they dragged Him to the cart that the fairies were sitting on. The soldiers heaved Him up and roughly dumped Him into the cart.

Jesus was unconscious.

Awinita quickly hopped off the edge and into the cart. She squatted next to Jesus. He was covered with sweat, dirt, and blood. One of His eyes had swollen shut.

As a soldier hooked up a mule to the cart, another came to check on Jesus—probably to see if He were still alive. Adahy quickly lifted Awinita out of the cart just as the soldier reached in and roughly shook Jesus. Jesus moaned, so the soldier was satisfied that He was alive. The cart jolted forward and the soldiers took Jesus back to Pilot. The ride was very bumpy, so the fairies flew the short distance back to the governor's porch.

*

Governor Pilot was upset and even more annoyed. He really did not want to crucify an innocent man. He knew the priests were behind this uprising. He knew that they were jealous of Jesus, because the people loved Him. They just wanted to be rid of Him, and they figured that he, the unpopular governor of their land, could do their dirty work for them.

Then Pilot's wife came to him and said, "You should not have any part of this. I have had a terrible nightmare, and I know this Man, Jesus, is innocent."

"I know He is too," Pilot agreed. "But these miserable priests are stirring up the people and I can't allow riots in the city. I have to do something or this dirty business will get out of hand."

A soldier came in and announced, "Sir, there're back."

Governor Pilot returned to the porch. The size of the mob in the courtyard had increased.

"We demand justice!" voices from the crowd called out, "Where is the blasphemer?"

"Crucify Him!"

Pilot raised his hands for them to quiet down. He motioned to a soldier off to the side and Jesus was brought in. Jesus was conscious but could barely stand. When the crowd saw Him, they all yelled out, "Crucify Him! Crucify Him!"

Confused, Awinita whispered to Adahy, "What does 'crucify' mean?"

"I don't know," Adahy replied, worried. "It doesn't sound good."

Pilot raised his voice, "See this Man?"

"Crucify Him!" the mob called out.

"I find no fault in Him! He has been punished, as you can see," Pilot tried to calm the crowd. "Now it is customary to release a prisoner in honor of your Passover. I wish to release this Man. He has suffered enough."

The priests had the crowd all fired up, and knowing the custom, they persuaded the crowd to ask for the release of another. The mob called out, "No! Release the prisoner Barabbas! Not this Man—a blasphemer—release Barabbas!"

"But Barabbas is a murderer!" Pilot yelled back.

"This Man is a blasphemer! We have a law and it demands that He die because He says that He is the Son of God!" the priests hollered back.

Pilot turned to Jesus, "What do You say for Yourself? These men accuse You! Defend Yourself against them!"

But Jesus said nothing, and Pilot was amazed. "Say something! Don't You know that I have the power to crucify You or release You?"

Just then Dustu blurted out, "Please say something!"

Awinita quickly put her hand over Dustu's mouth. "Shuush!" she whispered anxiously. Thankfully, no one noticed the small voice among the noisy crowd.

Jesus finally spoke and answered, "You only have that power because God has given it to you. The ones who have delivered Me to you have the greater sin."

Pilot wanted to release Jesus, but the unrest of the mob was getting worse. "Release Barabbas! Crucify Jesus!"

"Are they crazy?" Dustu whispered anxiously. "They want to release a murderer?"

"I think you're right." Adahy shook his head. "They are crazy."

The priests called to Pilot, "If you let this Man go, you are against Caesar, because this Man says He is the King!"

Pilot was worried now. He didn't want it said that he allowed someone to claim to be the king, because Caesar was the Roman king over all the land. So Pilot called out the priests, "You said He was the king of the Jews. So you want me to crucify *your* king?"

Then the clever priests answered, "We have only one king, and he is Caesar."

Then Pilot realized that he had to let them have their way or risk riots in the streets. So, he walked over to a basin of water and dipped his hands in it as if washing them. Then he said to them all, "I am innocent of the blood of this good Man. You will have your way."

The soldiers took the purple robe off Jesus and put His own clothes back on Him. They then took Him to be crucified.

Chapter 34

The Crucifixion

The mob followed the soldiers as they walked to the place called Calvary. Jesus was too weak to carry the wooden beam that they would crucify Him on, so a soldier grabbed a muscular man from the crowd and made him carry it.

The fairies flew from one roof-top to another, following the procession of people. As the mob walked through the streets of Jerusalem, many of the people cried out, "What are you doing? This is Jesus, the Blessed One!"

Others called out, "He is guilty of blasphemy! He must be crucified!"

And so it went—some calling out in anguish and others cheering. By the time the crowd reached the outskirts of Jerusalem, it had grown to a huge number of people. The word had spread of what was being done to Jesus, and the people who loved Him joined the crowd along with those who wanted Him dead. The people who loved Jesus were crying with great sorrow. The ones who wanted Him dead were cheering and mocking Him.

The mass of people approached a hill at Calvary. It was called Golgotha—the skull. It was an ugly barren place of rocks and dirt, and nearly no greenery. Already there were two thieves, and they were being nailed to a cross of two wooden beams. They screamed as the nails were hammered through their hands and feet. Then the wood was heaved up. The base of the cross slid into a narrow hole in the ground. As it was raised fully upright, the cross settled into the hole with a sickening thud.

The fairies flew to a nearly leafless branch of a lone tree at the hilltop. Seeing the two screaming men on the crosses, their eyes grew wide with horror at understanding what a crucifixion actually was. Dustu gasped in disbelief, "Are they going to do that to Jesus?"

Awinita's voice trembled as she answered, "I think so."

The fairies watched incredulously as Jesus was stripped of his clothes and was laid down onto the wood beam. Adahy was shaking his head as he watched a Roman soldier take four long black nails and knelt next to Jesus. Awinita tried to shield Dustu's eyes as the Roman pounded a nail through Jesus' hand and into the wood. Then he nailed in His other hand. Jesus moaned loudly with the awful pain. After that they put nails on His feet and hammered them in. Then they heaved up the wood. Jesus now hung on a cross between the two thieves.

The fairies watched the awful scene with tears streaming down their faces. They could hardly believe what they were seeing. They could never have ever imagined such cruelty!

The crowd stood in front of Jesus. Some were still mocking Him, but most of the sounds were of crying from those who loved Him. As Jesus hung there, the sky grew dark and the wind picked up. Even the sky looked horrified at the scene below. Jesus, despite his agony, looked up to heaven and said, "Father, forgive them because they don't know what they are doing."

Dustu heard Jesus say that and couldn't believe it. "After what they have just done to Him, He asks God to FORGIVE THEM?? I would have asked God to KILL them!"

"Dustu," Awinita wiped at her tears with the back of her hand and then put her arm around his shoulders, "He is Jesus. He loves everyone, even these horrible men who are doing this."

"It *is* hard for us to understand such love," Adahy added. "But He is so much more than we are. He is the Son of a loving God."

Then the soldiers put a sign on the top of Jesus' cross that read in three languages: "King of the Jews." The soldiers who had nailed Jesus up on the wooden cross took His robe and decided that it was a very nice one, even though it was covered in blood. So, they decided to gamble to see which one of them would win it.

Some cruel people began to mock Jesus again as He hung in terrible pain up on the cross. "Hey! You say You are the Son of God, so prove it! Come down off the cross!"

The priests also mocked Him, "You saved others, now save Yourself! If You are the King of Israel, come down off that cross and then we'll believe You!"

They laughed and taunted, "You said You are the Son of God, so let God Himself come and rescue You!"

Dustu was furious with the mockers. Here was Jesus, helpless and in agony, and yet they still insulted Him. Dustu looked around for something to throw at them, but found nothing. He was about to fly up higher into the scraggly tree to maybe find something there, but Awinita grabbed his arm, stopping him. "I know you are angry about this like I am, but we cannot interfere. Jesus is in control of everything."

Dustu shook his arm free and frowned. "I know, but I feel like we should do something against these mean people."

"I understand," Awinita agreed. "But it is not our place. This is Jesus, the Son of God. He knew what was to happen."

One of the two thieves, who were crucified with Jesus, moaned and cried in agony. He gasped out to Jesus, "If You really are the Christ, save Yourself and us!"

The other turned his head in pain and said, "What's wrong with you! Don't insult God. We are guilty of crimes but this Man is innocent." Then he asked Jesus, "Lord, please remember me when You enter Your kingdom."

Jesus turned His head toward him. "Truthfully I tell you," He gasped. "Today you will be with Me in paradise!"

A group of men and women forced themselves through the large crowd. They arrived at the front and one woman, an older woman who was still quite beautiful, collapsed to her knees when she saw Jesus, and cried out.

The other women with her wailed with sorrow when they saw Him. The beautiful older woman forced herself up from her knees and staggered to the base of the cross. Sobbing, she reached up to touch Jesus' feet but a soldier forced her away.

"Leave her alone!" some in the crowd called out angrily. "She is Mary, His mother!"

When Awinita heard that the woman was Jesus' mother, she was overwhelmed with new sorrow. With tears in her eyes, she turned to Adahy and asked, "Take me down to her."

"No," Adahy shook his head. "It's too dangerous with all these people so close."

As he said that, one of Jesus' Disciples ran to her and helped her up. Jesus gasped out in pain to him, "John, she is your mother now. Care for her."

The sky was now very dark. Above, the clouds whipped ferociously about as if they were terribly angry. The wind howled and blew harshly, whipping at the robes of the mob. The branch of the tree that the fairies sat upon rocked up and down with gusts of wind. Adahy put his arms around Awinita and Dustu, trying to protect them as the branch swayed violently.

Suddenly the sky lit up along with a loud crack of lightning! The air seemed full of energy and had a strange smell. The wind tugged at their wings as the tree branch swayed even more.

A powerful gust of wind pulled Dustu from Adahy's grasp! "Aaahhh!" Dustu screamed as he was tossed into the angry air.

"Dustu!" Awinita and Adahy both cried out in panic.

They watched helplessly as Dustu tumbled over and over in the wind, and then fell to the ground. In all the area of the hard-packed dirt ground on skull hill, there was one—only one—clump of grass. To the fairies amazement, Dustu landed softly on that very one grass clump—unhurt.

Stunned, with the wind still blowing ferociously, Dustu looked up from the ground and toward the branch where Adahy and Awinita still struggled to cling to. He knew—with no doubt in his mind—that Jesus, in spite of His pain, had saved him from the fall. Adahy and Awinita knew it as well. It was a miracle.

*

The time had arrived. Jesus lifted His head and called out, "My God, My God! Have You forgotten Me?" Then He said with His last breath, "It is finished. Father, into Your hands I send My spirit."

His head fell forward.

Jesus was dead.

Those who loved Jesus screamed and cried out. The fairies also cried out, not caring if anyone heard them. Awinita turned to Adahy and buried her face into his chest, crying. As he held her close, she could feel his tears dripping onto her cheek.

Suddenly the ground began to shake. Dustu, still lying on the grass clump, jumped up and awkwardly flew back to Awinita and Adahy. The three of them held tightly to the branch as the tree shook from side to side. Then they heard terrible cracking sounds all around them. Dustu looked down to the ground and saw that the rocks below were splitting open!

"Look!" he shouted. "The rocks are breaking apart!"

Many in the crowd had fallen to the ground as it shook underneath them. They screamed in terror as the rocks and the ground split around them.

(At that moment in the great temple of Jerusalem, the very heavy veil across the most Holy room—where the golden Ark of the Covenant sat—split down the center!)

The Roman officer, a Centurion who was in charge of the crucifixion, was amazed and said, "Truly this Man was the Son of God!"

Chapter 35

He is Dead

The wind died down as quickly as it had come up and the earth no longer shook. The people began to get up off the ground, murmuring to each other in wonder of it all. The fairies, still huddled together on the branch, looked down at the cracked ground littered with split-open rocks. Hearing orders being given, they watched as a Roman soldier picked up a length of wood and walked toward the crosses.

(Because the Sabbath day was near, the priests had wanted the prisoners off the crosses as soon as possible. So, they had asked Governor Pilot if the soldiers could break the legs of the crucified men to make them die quicker. Pilot had agreed.)

Adahy nudged Awinita and pointed. With alarm she asked, "What do you think that man is going to do with that piece of wood?"

Before Adahy could answer, the soldier swung the wood and smashed the legs of one of the thieves, breaking them. The man screamed out in even more agony. Then the soldier went to the other terrified thief and swung the wood at his legs. The fairies could hear the crack of his bones as his legs also broke.

Horrified, Dustu exclaimed, "He's going to hit Jesus!"

"It won't matter, Dustu," Adahy said sadly as he looked at Jesus' body hanging limply on the cross. "They can't hurt Him anymore."

The soldier turned to Jesus but saw that He was already dead, so he didn't break His bones. Instead, to be sure He was dead, he took a spear and stabbed Jesus in the side. Out of the large gash came blood and water.

Awinita covered her eyes. She didn't know how much more she could endure. After a short while, the fairies watched as the mob began to disperse. Those who hated Jesus left with satisfaction. They had accomplished their desire to get rid of Him. Those who loved and respected Jesus, left with heavy hearts. The fairies, still in shock at all they had witnessed, remained in the tree after most of the people had left.

(During the crucifixion, one good elderly man had gone to Governor Pilot and had asked for the body of Jesus so he could bury Him. Pilot had agreed.)

The body of Jesus was taken down off the cross and carefully carried away. Mary and the other women, plus the followers of Jesus, walked sadly beside and behind Him. The fairies, wondering what they were going to do with Jesus, followed along.

The good elderly man led the group to a new tomb—a small cave. The body of Jesus was wrapped in fine linen and placed in the cave, and then several strong men rolled a heavy round rock across the front of it—sealing it.

*

The fairies followed Mary and the Disciples to a house at the edge of the city. They settled in an open window sill. Seeing Mary's grief, Awinita whispered to Adahy, "I wish I could help ease her pain."

Adahy shook his head sadly and said, "I don't think anything can ease her pain, but you can try." He scooped up Awinita and flew her to where Mary sat. He set Awinita on the back of the chair, and then hovered behind her ready to catch her in case she was to fall off.

Awinita, invisible, sat next to Mary. She touched Mary gently and tried to soothe some of her pain, but it was impossible. Mary could not be comforted. She and the others all mourned throughout the rest of the day and into the night.

*

The fairies were very tired and decided to fly to the roof to try to get some sleep. They rolled out their sleeping mats and settled down upon them. They didn't have much of an appetite, so they ate a small meal of figs and a few nuts. Dustu, still angry about all that had happened, had spread out his mat a bit away from Awinita and Adahy.

Awinita, rolled over and leaned in Adahy's direction. She whispered, "I'm worried about Dustu. He's so angry; he keeps losing people important to him."

Adahy took her hand and tried to sound reassuring, "He'll be OK. Everything we have witnessed would be tough on even the strongest fairies."

Awinita rolled back and looked up into the starry night sky and whispered sadly, "What we have seen here in this land makes no sense. I miss home. The forest, our friends ... even that grouchy old brown bear."

Adahy chuckled, "So do I. We'll start for home soon ... after we gather some food. I promise, we'll be back there before you know it."

*

The fairies woke to banging and loud voices coming from beneath them in the house.

"Let me in! I have news!" the door pounder exclaimed.

The fairies quickly flew down to the window to listen better.

Peter opened the door and a young man stumbled in. He plopped down onto a rug and gasped out breathlessly, "You'll never guess what happened to that betrayer, Judas!"

"Take a moment," Peter said to the young man as he began to catch his breath. "So, what happened?"

"We know that Judas was paid 30 pieces of silver to lead the priest's men to Jesus, but I found out that he later repented. He went back to them and said that he had sinned by betraying an innocent Man. The priests didn't care that Jesus was innocent. Can you believe that? They *knew* He was innocent and went ahead with their plans to kill Him! Anyway, when Judas heard that, he threw the money down at their feet and left!"

"Really!" the men listened, surprised.

"That's not the end of the story. Judas went and hung himself! He's dead!"

Chapter 36

He is Gone!

In spite of their success in crucifying Jesus, the jealous priests were still not satisfied. They had heard that Jesus told His Disciples that He would be crucified and that even though He were dead, He would rise—be alive again—after three days. So, they went to Pilot and asked him to assign soldiers to guard the tomb of Jesus. They figured that His Disciples might come and steal His body and then tell everyone that He had risen from the dead. That would surely, they told Pilot, result in riots. So, soldiers were stationed at the tomb to keep watch. The tomb was also sealed with wax seals—so to show whether or not it had been opened.

During the last two days, the fairies had been busy gathering supplies for the long trip home. Then it was the morning of the third day.

A woman named Mary Magdalene and another woman walked into the garden where Jesus' tomb was located. They could see the two Roman guards sitting relaxed on the ground near it. As the women approached, the earth began to tremble! The two frightened women clung to each other to keep their balance. Suddenly, a bright light shown from all around the tomb!

Then, to their amazed eyes, a mighty Angel descended from heaven above. His feet touched the ground in front of the tomb. He was dressed in pure white and his face glowed with an amazing light. He looked directly at the Roman guards. They were so terrified that they fainted!

The two shocked women stood there and watched the Angel roll the great stone away from the tomb entrance. The women cowered in fear and bowed low before him, but the Angel said to them, "Don't be afraid. I know you are here for Jesus of Nazareth who was crucified. He is not here anymore, so don't seek the living among the dead of this cemetery. He has risen from death, just like He told everyone. Remember? He said to you that He would be delivered into the hands of sinful men and be crucified, but on the third day He would rise." The magnificent Angel motioned toward the open tomb, "Come and see for yourselves."

The women warily walked toward the tomb, bent over, and looked inside. It was empty! Then the Angel said, "Go and tell Peter and all the Disciples that He is alive and will see them soon."

The women ran from the tomb with a mixture of fear at what they had just seen and also great joy. The Angel had said that Jesus has risen from the dead! They ran to the house where the Disciples were and burst through the door.

Out of sight on the roof, the fairies were filling a bag with some dates. They heard commotion within the house—excited voices of the two women as they excitedly told the Disciples what they had seen.

Listening intently, Awinita looked at Adahy and asked incredulously, "Did she just say that an Angel told her that Jesus is alive?"

"Yes! That's what I heard too!" Adahy exclaimed.

"Me too!" Dustu shouted excitedly.

Not really believing the women, all the Disciples jumped up and ran to the tomb. Excited, Adahy scooped up Awinita and the three fairies followed them. Could Jesus really be alive?

When the group arrived at the tomb, Peter was shocked to see that the great stone had indeed been rolled away. He bent over and entered the tomb. There he saw the linen cloth that had covered the body of Jesus—all folded up, and next to that was the linen cloth that had covered Jesus' head. He was amazed and wondered what had happened.

Each of the men peered into the empty tomb, seeing for themselves that it was indeed empty. The invisible fairies hovered at the entrance of the tomb and then they too flew in. Inside the cool cave, they too saw the folded burial linens—but not Jesus. He was gone!

Peter and the others anxiously talked over each other wondering and guessing that perhaps someone had stolen the body of Jesus. Adahy carried Awinita out of the tomb and they sat down on the top of the great stone which had been rolled away. Dustu flew down to the ground and tried to push the heavy stone.

"What on earth are you doing?" Awinita asked.

"I think that a strong Angel moved this stone. It's way too heavy for anyone else," Dustu grunted as he pushed again.

"Dustu, you can't ..."

"Look!" Adahy interrupted. "The people are leaving. Let's go."

The Disciples left, confused and worried, and the fairies followed them. No one noticed that Mary Magdalene remained by the tomb, kneeling down, and crying.

After a while, Mary Magdalene wiped her cheeks with the back of her hand and stood up. She walked the few steps to the tomb, bent down, and looked inside. Suddenly, two Angels appeared!

One sat where Jesus' head would have been and one sat where His feet would have been. One Angel said to her, "Woman, why do you weep?"

She shakily answered, "Because my Lord has been taken away and I don't know where He is." Then she backed away from the tomb and saw a man, who she thought was the cemetery gardener, standing there.

The gardener said to her, "Miss, why do you weep? Who are you looking for?"

She answered, "Sir, if you have taken Jesus, please tell me where He is."

Then the man (who she thought was the gardener) said lovingly, "Mary."

In shock, she realized that He was Jesus! "Master!" she cried out with joy and fell to her knees. Then He disappeared.

Chapter 37

He is Alive!

The fairies sat on a window sill listening to the Disciples discuss the morning events. Suddenly Mary Magdalene was banging on the door. She saw an eye in the peep-hole. "Let me in!" she shouted. "Let me in! He's alive!"

The door opened. "He's alive!" she breathlessly exclaimed. "I saw Him! He's alive! He really is!"

The men just looked at her, and then one shook his head and said, "Mary, it has been a stressful morning. Are you seeing things?"

"No! I saw Him!" she anxiously looked over all the men. "I really saw Him! He spoke to me. It was really Him!"

"My dear," Peter said softly. "We all mourn. You just let your imagination get the best of you."

"Come and sit down, and have something to eat," another comforted her as he led her to a chair.

"You don't believe me," she said sadly. "Why don't you believe me?" Then she began to cry.

The doors were shut and locked because the Disciples were afraid. They had gotten word that the tomb guards had gone to the priests and told them what had happened. The priests gathered together and decided to pay the soldiers a large amount of money so that they would keep their mouths shut and say that Jesus' followers had come and stolen His body while they slept. The priests also promised the soldiers that if Governor Pilot found out, they would support their false story so Pilot wouldn't punish them. The high priest then ordered that the Disciples be hunted and found, so that they couldn't tell anyone about Jesus being raised from the dead.

*

They all sat, eating dinner. The fairies sat up on the rafters and ate their dinner as well. There was plenty of food, so they borrowed some when no one was looking.

Suddenly, Jesus appeared! He said, "Peace be to you."

"Aaahhhh!" the men shouted out in shock, some falling backward off their chairs. "A ghost!"

The sudden appearance of Jesus startled the fairies as well. Dustu was so surprised that he dropped a piece of bread that he was eating. It fell down to the table below them, but no one sitting there noticed.

They all stared at Jesus and then He said to them, "What's wrong? Don't you believe it's Me? Why do you think I'm a ghost? Does a ghost have flesh and bones? Look at Me. Touch Me. See My hands and feet? See the nail holes?"

With their mouths hanging open in amazement, one by one realized He was among them. Alive! They fell to their knees before Him and worshipped Him.

Then Jesus said to them, "Why didn't you believe that I had risen from the dead? I told you before that I would have to suffer greatly, be killed, and then rise from death on the third day." He paused and then asked, "Got anything to eat?"

*

The fairies remained hidden in the rafters as they watched Jesus eat a piece of broiled fish and some honeycomb with His Disciples. After dinner, He suddenly disappeared from their sight. Everyone sat there with their mouths hanging open in amazement—again.

"Where did He go?" they asked as they looked all around.

Adahy rose up from his perch in the rafters and whispered to Awinita, "I'm going outside to see if I can find Jesus."

"I'm coming too!" Dustu declared.

"All right, let's go."

Together they made themselves invisible and flew out of a window. They flew all around the house, but Jesus was nowhere to be seen. They returned to the rafter and landed next to Awinita. Dustu was very discouraged. He still desperately wanted Jesus to bring Waya back from the dead. He also wanted to ask Him to bring back his and Awinita's father as well. He figured if you are going to ask for one miracle, why not ask for two?

One of Jesus' Disciples, Thomas, had not been there when Jesus had appeared. When he finally returned to the house, the others told him of the miraculous appearance. Jesus was alive! But Thomas didn't believe them. He said, "I'm sorry, but I just can't believe that. The only way I'll believe that Jesus is alive is if I can touch the nail holes in His hands and feet, and feel the wound in His side."

*

The fairies sat on the roof, hoping that Jesus would appear again. "It's been eight days, Dustu," Adahy said. "We'll need to start for home soon."

187

"But we can't. Not yet. I have to talk to Him. We can't leave until we see Him again," Dustu pleaded.

"I know how you feel, Dustu, but He may not come back," Awinita said sadly. "We can't stay here forever."

Awinita wanted to speak to Jesus as much as Dustu did. As they were discussing how much longer they should wait, they heard the most wonderful voice coming from inside the house. The voice said, "Peace be with you."

Dustu's eyes widened and he exclaimed, "It's Him! He's back!" Dustu jumped up and flew down to the window. Adahy and Awinita were right behind him.

They landed on the window sill and heard Jesus say to the unbelieving Disciple, "Thomas, touch My hands and My side … and believe."

Thomas gasped, "My Lord! My God! It *is* You!"

Jesus said to him, "Because you have seen Me with your own eyes, you believe. Blessed are those who have *not* seen Me, but believe anyway." Then Jesus told them, "Tell My followers to go into the land of Galilee, and there they will all see Me."

And then He was gone again.

"Oh, no!" Dustu moaned, "He's gone again."

"Yes," Awinita put her hand on his arm, "but He said where we should go to see Him again."

"So what are we waiting for?" Dustu said eagerly. "Let's go!"

Chapter 38

The Ascension

As they were told to do, the Disciples traveled into the area of Galilee. The fairies flew along with them, stopping frequently to rest. Even though he was very strong, it was tiring for Adahy to carry Awinita for hours upon hours.

On the way, the group stopped by a lake. Peter and the other Disciples decided they wanted to go fishing, so they borrowed a small fishing boat. Dustu told Awinita that he wanted to go with them to see how they caught fish. Adahy told Awinita that he would go as well to make sure Dustu stayed out of trouble. Awinita smiled and agreed. She sat in a tree on the shore and waited for them to return.

The men fished all night, but caught nothing. Morning came, and they saw a Man standing on the shore. The Man called out to them, "Did you catch any fish?"

They called back to the stranger, "No, nothing."

The voices awoke Dustu and Adahy as they had fallen asleep in the corner of the boat.

Then the stranger called back to the men, "Throw your net out on the right hand side of the boat and try."

They did as the stranger on the shore suggested, and to their shock, the net became full of fish! Dustu and Adahy were amazed to see all the fish flipping about within the net.

"It's the Lord!" John exclaimed.

"What?" Dustu and Adahy looked toward the shore. Adahy smiled, "It's Him, Dustu."

With great joy, Peter jumped into the water and swam to shore. Dustu and Adahy eagerly flew along above him. When they got there, they saw that Jesus had loaves of bread plus a fire burning brightly in a fire-pit.

Adahy and Dustu joined Awinita in the tree. "How long has He been here?" Dustu asked Awinita.

"He hasn't ... He wasn't ... He just appeared. Fire pit and all!" Awinita answered in amazement.

Dustu frowned, "But you could have spoken to Him while He was alone. Now He won't be alone at all."

"No Dustu," Awinita tried to explain. "He appeared just a second before He called out to the men in the boat. There wasn't enough time."

Jesus again called out to the men, "Bring in the fish!" Peter helped drag in the heavy net. It held 153 fish, but yet the net wasn't broken.

Then Jesus said to them, "Let's eat!"

The group had a joyous reunion with the Lord Jesus. The fairies sat together up in the tree and ate from the food they had brought along. They desperately hoped they would be able to find a few moments when Jesus was alone so they could talk to Him. But, to their dismay, just after breakfast Jesus suddenly disappeared again.

"Not again!" Dustu groaned. "Not again."

The Disciples gathered their supplies, and then traveled onward in Galilee. The fairies quietly followed along with them.

*

Word had spread that the followers of Jesus were traveling in Galilee, and people who loved Jesus began to joint them. Very soon, there was a crowd traveling with them. The large group stopped to rest at the bottom of a small hill. A bit away, the fairies sat upon the top of a rock.

Suddenly, Jesus appeared! Everyone gasped and fell to their knees, calling out, "Master! Lord!"

"He's back!" Dustu said excitedly.

Jesus looked across the crowd and then to His Disciples. He began to speak to them, "You have been witnesses to all. Now, go back to Jerusalem and wait there for the Holy Spirit to come to you. After that, then go and preach the gospel to every creature in all the nations. Teach them to observe all that I have said. Tell them to repent of their sins and be baptized in the name of the Father, Son, and the Holy Spirit.

"He who believes in Me and is baptized will be saved, and he who doesn't believe in Me will be damned. All power has been given to Me over heaven and earth." He lovingly looked over them all and said, "Know that I am with you always, even until the end of the world."

Then a mist of pure white began to swirl around His feet. His smiling gaze passed over the amazed people. Then, to the fairies utter amazement, His gentle eyes turned directly toward them. He smiled and thought to them, "Be saddened no longer." Then His kind gaze settled on Dustu. "Take comfort in My words. Your father is in our heavenly home ... as is Waya and his wife. They are all alive and happy in My realm. You will see them again one day in the future, when you also come home."

A sudden peace filled Dustu's heart, chasing away all the sorrow and anger. Awinita and Adahy both gasped ... the incredible peace washed across their hearts as well.

The clouds about Jesus thickened. He raised His hands and the clouds began to rise, carrying Him with them into the sky. The stunned crowd watched in amazed silence until He was out of sight. Then two magnificent Angels appeared and said to the people, "As you have seen Him leave, so shall He come again." Then they too disappeared.

The fairies were stunned. He had spoken to them! He knew they were there! Dustu had tears running down his cheeks. He knew that Waya would not be coming back to him, but now he *knew* that his friend was happy and in heaven with God. Then he realized that even though they had never gotten the chance to talk to Jesus, He knew Waya's name. Dustu then realized that Jesus had known all along about Waya!

The people turned to one another and cried out with joy and wonder. They sang and praised Jesus! Over the loud rejoicing voices, Awinita heard a gasp behind her.

"Your wing!" Dustu exclaimed. "It's ... it's ..."

Adahy interrupted in amazement, "It's healed! Your wing is whole again!"

Stunned, Awinita twisted her head back and saw the tip of her new wing. "Oh!" she cried out. "The Lord has healed me!" She reached back and touched her beautiful new wing. Tears of emotion filled her eyes. "He healed me!"

Adahy and Dustu hugged her with joy.

"See if you can fly!" Adahy exclaimed eagerly as he released his hug.

Awinita fluttered both her delicate wings together for the first time in a very long while. She easily rose up into the air. The sunlight seemed to dance with rainbow colors across her wings.

Then, giggling, she flew in circles above. Adahy and Dustu dropped their packs to the ground and joyfully rose into the air and joined her.

Adahy took her hand and they raced to the top of the hill. Dustu flew up next to them as they hovered high above. With her other hand, Awinita reached for her brother. Holding hands, they all looked to heaven and called out, "Oh, thank You Lord Jesus! Thank You! Thank You!"

Chapter 39

Starting Home

Their quest had ended. They left home to find the Savior, Jesus. Even though they were too late to hear Him teach, they had learned so much from the stories told by others. Now it was time to return to their own homeland and tell everyone all they had learned—just as Jesus had told everyone to do as He rose to heaven.

They followed the Disciples back to Jerusalem and searched for a caravan returning to the area where they had left the ark. Finally they found one. There, hooked up to a small cart, they recognized a young donkey. It was Ayir, Chamor's nephew! He was the young donkey who had carried Jesus into Jerusalem.

They greeted him, but he hung his head and said nothing. Adahy tried again, "Hi Ayir, we know your uncle Chamor. He was very kind to give us a ride into Jerusalem."

"So what," he muttered in his thought answer.

Surprised at his surly attitude, Awinita thought to him, "What's wrong?"

"Nothing," he snarled back.

"Something has to be wrong," Awinita thought soothingly, "You seem miserable."

"You'd be miserable too if you killed the Holy One of God!"

Stunned, all three fairies gasped, "What??"

"Are your thoughts deaf? I said that I killed the Holy One of God! Jesus the Christ!"

"What on earth are you talking about? You didn't kill Him!" Adahy replied, astonished.

"I certainly did!" Ayir's thoughts raged. "I carried Him into Jerusalem, on MY back! I carried Him to His death! It's my fault!" Then he began to cry.

"Oh Ayir!" Awinita flew over to him and put her hand on his head and comforted him, "No, you didn't kill Him. You had the honor to carry Him, that's all. We know that you had nothing to do with His death. We were there! We heard Jesus say that He knew that He would be falsely accused and crucified, and then He would rise from death after three days!"

"Rise from death?" Ayir asked with astonishment as he raised his head. "You say that He's a ... alive??"

"Yes, He is!" All three fairies exclaimed together.

"I don't understand."

"We were there! We saw it all! He is alive from death! And now He is in heaven with Father God, and He will return someday. He promised!"

Ayir was silent for a moment, then he asked, "Then I didn't kill Him?"

"No!" the fairies all shouted out together and then they laughed with joy. "He's not dead!"

*

The caravan was about to leave. The fairies had gathered supplies as best they could. Ayir was happy to have them ride along in his cart. A great weight of sorrow was now lifted off him. He was so happy that he was blameless in the horror of Jesus' death.

The caravan began its long trip. It passed by the olive grove where Adahy, Awinita, and Dustu had met the other fairies. They saw the young girls and waved to them as they passed by. The girls sighed as they waved back to Adahy and watched him leave.

Awinita smiled to herself … she couldn't help it.

*

The caravan arrived at the first oasis without incident. The next day as they traveled toward the second oasis, they kept watch for any bandits, but thankfully none appeared. They arrived late at the second oasis, but still took their time in visiting the mice and telling them all that they had seen and heard. The mice listened with great interest. They were dismayed with Jesus being betrayed and murdered, then happy again at the Resurrection and Ascension.

The caravan traveled to the third oasis, where their journey had begun. Needing a ride, the fairies flew around the camp until they heard of someone who was going back to the little town. The same town where they had left Bullox and Brutus, the two kind oxen who had carried them from the merchant piers.

It was nearly dark when they arrived. They immediately flew to the barn at the edge of town. There they were! Inside the barn was Bullox and Brutus, enjoying a meal of fresh grain.

"Hello!" the three fairies called out to their friends.

Bullox's head jerked up. "Who said that?"

"It's us!" Dustu called back.

"It's Awinita, Adahy, and Dustu!" Brutus nodded his great head.

"We're glad to see you back again, and safely," Bullox welcomed them.

"Wait a moment. Didn't the little lady have a broken wing?" Brutus asked, surprised, as the three fairies hovered in front of them.

"Yes, I did. It had been burned in a fire," Awinita reminded him.

"But Jesus healed it!" Dustu exclaimed. "It's OK now, and she can fly!"

"Incredible!" Brutus said in amazement.

"So you found Jesus!" Bullox nodded his head. "Tell us all about it, please!"

So, the fairies told the oxen the whole story, and they believed it all. After a meal of grain and nuts, they all settled down to sleep. The next morning, Bullox noticed something. "Awinita, last time you were here, you had a nightmare about the great fire that you told us about. But last night, you didn't seem to have any bad dreams at all. I'm a light sleeper, so I would have noticed."

Awinita thought for a moment. "You're right! I haven't had a nightmare about that since Jesus healed my wing!" She said happily. "He must have healed me from having nightmares, too!"

"I'm glad to hear that," Bullox nodded his head.

"I'm glad to hear that too," Adahy grinned. "So I guess you won't need that piece of rose quartz stone anymore."

"Maybe, but I will always love it," Awinita said, smiling up at him. "That's because you gave it to me."

A big smile lit up Adahy's face.

Chapter 40

Back to the Ark

The fairies rode with Bullox and Brutus back to the merchant piers. They said their good-byes and thanked the oxen for all their help. Then, they eagerly gathered their bags and flew to Mr. Jericho's warehouse. Through the open doors they saw him, working on a boat.

"Mr. Jericho!" they all three called out to him as they flew inside.

He turned and smiled widely to see his fairy friends again. "Oh my!" he exclaimed. "You're back! How wonderful!" Then he saw Awinita fluttering her wings, hovering in the air along with Adahy and Dustu. His eyes opened wide with surprise, "Your wing! It's healed! You must have found Jesus!"

*

The fairies stayed with Mr. Jericho several days, resting up for the long voyage home. As he worked on a boat, he listened intently on the stories of their journey. He was deeply saddened by the news of the Crucifixion, but overjoyed at the Resurrection and Ascension. Also, each time he heard of a miracle performed by Jesus, he would exclaim, "Blessed is the Lord!" He ended up saying that a lot ….

*

When it was nearing the time to leave, the fairies asked some seagulls to search for the dolphins, Tinka, Binka, Finn, or Chipper. Chipper was the first to be found so he went in search for Marco. Thankfully, Marco had not gone too far out into the ocean so Chipper soon found him. Marco graciously volunteered again for the long and tiresome voyage back.

Mr. Jericho had refinished the bottom of the ark so that it was in tip-top shape for the trip. He re-tarred the roof so that it was now extra water-tight. He also put new water barrels in the ark as well.

Mr. Jericho had made arrangement with the local merchants to buy a good supply of smoked fish, dried fruits and vegetables, grains, and nuts. Dustu told him how good sweet-dates were, so he made a special effort to include a large package of them.

Adahy, Awinita, and Dustu thanked Mr. Jericho for all his help and kindness. They said that they wished they could somehow re-pay him, but he said that the wonderful stories of Jesus they had told him were worth far more than his efforts.

*

The day had come. Tinka, Binka, and Finn had also heard that the ark was ready to go. They swam with Chipper into the harbor at dusk, and waited.

"Mr. Jericho, you have been a wonderful friend to us," Adahy said, holding out his hand to Mr. Jericho.

Mr. Jericho bent over and carefully shook Adahy's hand, "As also you have been to me. I wish you a safe journey."

"Yes," Dustu added, "thank you very much … especially for the dates."

"You are very welcome, my young friend," Mr. Jericho answered as he gently shook Dustu's small outstretched hand.

Awinita smiled and rose up into the air to give Mr. Jericho a kiss on the cheek, "Thank you so much for everything."

"Oh, my," Mr. Jericho chuckled. "How nice to be given a kiss by such a lovely young lady!"

"How nice to have a friend such as you," she whispered back.

The fairies flew onto the deck of the ark. Mr. Jericho unlashed the ropes that kept the boat close to his pier. The dolphins picked up the straps in the water and slowly began to pull the boat out into the harbor. The fairies waved good-bye as their boat slowly moved away. The darkness quickly grew and soon they could no longer see Mr. Jericho waving at them from the pier.

Chapter 41

War with the Romans

Marco lay low in the water beyond the harbor, waiting. The dolphins were exhausted by the time they found him.

"Pulling this thing is hard!" Chipper complained.

"Not for me," Marco laughed.

"I guess not, since you are about a hundred times bigger than we are," Binka laughed.

"Not quite a hundred times, but …"

A voice interrupted, calling out from the dark water, "We heard that you are returning to your homeland. We will assist you as far as we can."

Hearing the sea-man's thoughts, the fairies rushed to the rail. "Hi!" They called to the sea-man.

"Hello, my friends," he answered as he raised his spear in salute. "It will be a long journey and some of my people will accompany you for as far as they can, especially through this dangerous part of the sea. These days the Roman ships seem more plentiful than usual."

"Thank you for your kindness." Adahy called back. "We are grateful for your help."

"You are welcome," the sea-man said. "We should try to get as far into the sea as we can before dawn."

"Yes," Marco agreed. "Let's get moving."

The dolphins transferred the pull-straps to Marco's mouth, and then they were on their way.

*

The fairies awoke to bright sunlight shining through the boat's windows. They feasted on a breakfast of hot boiled grains and sweet dates. (Dustu was overjoyed to see how many Mr. Jericho had packed for them!) Afterward, they all went out onto the deck.

"Marco?" Adahy thought-called out.

"Yes," Marco thought back. "I'm here."

"How are you? How was your night?"

"I'm fine," Marco answered. "We have traveled quite a good distance already. I'm glad the sea-man suggested that we travel at night, because we passed quite a few Roman ships. I think we are far enough along that we may not see many more."

"I'm glad to hear that," Adahy agreed. "Are you tired? Do you want to rest awhile or go and find food? You've been pulling all night."

"Oh, thank you, but no. I did get something to eat earlier, while you were all asleep."

"I'm glad to hear tha ..."

Suddenly Adahy was interrupted. "Roman ship!" a sea-man called out. "Heading this way!"

"Oh no! What do we do?"

Tinka, Binka, Finn, and Chipper came to the surface of the water. "I have an idea!" Chipper thought out. "We'll call the seagulls to fly at the ship! So maybe the Romans will turn and go another way!"

"Great idea!" Marco called out. "Tell the gulls that I will reward them with lots of fish!"

The dolphins quickly disappeared under the waves and headed for the shore where the seagulls lived. Awinita and Dustu ran to the railing of the boat and looked for the Roman ship. Then they all flew to the roof to get a better view. There it was! A ship with its colorful sails full of wind, heading right at them—and coming fast!

"They must have seen us! They're coming to investigate our strange looking boat!" Adahy exclaimed anxiously.

"I'm going to pull the boat toward the shore! I can't go too close, but I can probably get closer than that big ship can!" Marco thought to them as he changed direction.

Suddenly a large flock of seagulls appeared and flew over the ark toward the Roman ship. Then more gulls came! And more! (The dolphins had done an excellent job of finding them!) The huge number of gulls surrounded the Roman ship, screeching and flying erratically around it. By now, the ship was close enough so that the fairies could hear the Roman soldiers yelling out! The squawking gulls flew at the men, weaving in and out of the masts and sails. The men swatted at them with whatever they could find, all the while screaming and cursing at the wild birds.

Dustu and Adahy cheered the gulls! "Poop on them!" Dustu yelled out in thought. "Get 'em! Poop on them!"

Then, to add to the confusion, the gulls did just that. Seagull poop rained down! Screaming, the soldiers scurried across the deck to find shelter from the stinky white globs that splashed down onto their heads.

Laughing, the fairies watched with delight as the ship quickly turned away and headed in the opposite direction. "Hurray!" They called out. "Hurray for the seagulls!"

Giggling, the dolphins returned. "We won a war with the Romans!" Finn cheered.

"We did it!" Tinka and Binka thought joyously.

"We have them on the run!" Chipper joined in.

"It really wasn't a 'war,'" Adahy tried to point out.

"Yeah!" Dustu exclaimed. "The Romans never even had a chance!"

"We can't thank you enough," Awinita called to the dolphins. "Chipper, that was a brilliant idea."

"Here come the gulls," Marco announced. "I need to fulfill my promise. Marco dropped the pull-straps and disappeared beneath the waves.

"We want our fish!" the gulls demanded as they flew around the ark. "We did what you wanted … it was lots of fun!"

Suddenly Marco's great shape surfaced and he blew water and small fish up into the air! The gulls madly flew to catch the fish before they dropped back into the sea.

"More! More!" they demanded, so Marco dove down into the depths … three more times!

The gulls were well fed, thank-you and good-byes were said, and the journey was back on course again. Soon, Marco had pulled the ark through and out of the Mediterranean Sea and into the Atlantic Ocean—the great sea.

After the ark was safely away from the land, the sea-people, the dolphins, and Marco spent many hours listening to the fairies as they told their story of finding Jesus and what had happened after that. They were wondrous at the miracles, horrified at the Crucifixion, amazed at Jesus' return from the dead, and heartened at the Ascension of Jesus into heaven. They said they would spread the word to whoever wanted to listen.

Chapter 42

Jokes

The days passed and everyone was getting bored. Dustu and Chipper passed time telling jokes.

"Why don't oysters share their pearls?" Chipper started.

"I don't know," Dustu responded. "Why don't they share their pearls?"

"Because they're shellfish!"

Then they both laughed.

"I don't get it," Marco joined in.

"It's a joke, Marco," Chipper explained. "They are shellfish and shellfish sounds like selfish. And if they don't share, then they are selfish. Do you get it now?"

"Hmmm," Marco said. "Tell another one."

"OK," Chipper laughed. "What does seaweed say when it is stuck at the bottom of the sea?"

"But seaweed doesn't talk," Marco remarked, puzzled.

"OK, so what does seaweed say when it's stuck on the bottom?" Dustu repeated, grinning.

"It says 'Kelp! Kelp!'" Chipper giggled.

"I still don't understand," Marco shook his mighty head. "Seaweeds don't talk and they are most always stuck to the bottom of the sea because they grow there."

A young sea-man swam up. "I don't understand either. What Chipper said was silly."

"They're jokes! They're supposed to be silly."

"OK, OK," Dustu interrupted. "I have one. Why do fish always know how much they weigh?"

"Because fish have scales!" Chipper answered gleefully.

"Right!" Dustu laughed. "They have scales!"

"Of course they have scales!" the young sea-man said with irritation. "We scrape them off or else they get caught in our teeth when we eat them. There's nothing funny about that!"

"No," Dustu grinned, "It's about the scales ... like to weigh something ... and fish have scales ... so it's a joke ...."

"I don't have scales," Marco said. "And I'm a fish."

"No, Marco, you are not a fish, not really," Adahy interrupted, as he and Awinita sat down next to Dustu. "You are a sea mammal."

More sea-men came to the surface of the water and joined in the conversation, "Neither then are we fish. We certainly do *not* have scales!"

"I agree," Adahy nodded his head toward them. "You are sea-people, not fish. Not fish at all."

"I have one!" Awinita smiled. Everyone turned toward Awinita as she asked, "What fish swims only at night?"

They all looked confused, so she gave the answer, "A star fish!"

"Yes!" Chipper and Dustu laughed. "That's a good one!"

The newly arrived sea-people looked confused. "Starfish swim in the daytime as well. So that is not particularly amusing."

"Wait a moment," the young sea-man said thoughtfully. "I think I get it. A star in the sky is only seen at night, and a starfish is a star... I see what you mean by "joke" but I still think it is all silly. Let's hear another one."

"OK," Chipper said. "Why does the whale cross the great sea?"

"He crosses the sea to get to the other side, of course!" one of the newly arrived sea-men answered.

"Yes!" Both Dustu and Chipper exclaimed together. "That's right! You got it!"

"But that's not funny. Why else would a whale cross the sea if he didn't want to get to the other side?"

"Perhaps he did that as a favor to several fairies?" Marco added wryly.

"But, that makes sense so why is it a joke? I still don't ..."

Suddenly another head broke through the surface. It was a sea-man who was very old. The other sea-men nodded their heads and raised their spears toward him in respect. "What is all this foolishness?" He asked sternly.

"Sir, we are telling jokes," the young sea-man answered respectfully.

"Jokes!" he scoffed. "Don't you youngsters have any more important things to do?"

"Please forgive them, sir," Adahy spoke up. "We are just having a bit of fun. Our friends have been working very hard to help keep us safe."

"Yes," the crusty old sea-man muttered. "That is what they are here for."

"Sir?" Dustu called to him. "Would you like to try one of our jokes?"

"Yes," the other sea-men eagerly joined together. "Sir, please try one!"

"Alright then," he gave in. "Let's hear one."

"Yes, sir. What did the boy octopus say to the girl octopus?"

"I haven't the remotest idea," the old sea-man answered.

"I want to hold your hand, hand, hand, hand, hand, hand, hand, hand."

"I get it!" the young sea-man exclaimed. "The octopus has eight arms!"

The old sea-man just scowled.

"I have another one!" Chipper announced eagerly. "What kind of fish chase mice?"

The sea-men just stared at Chipper, and then one said, "None!"

"Wait! I got it!" Dustu shouted out. "A cat-fish!"

"Catfish do not eat mice!" the old sea-man blurted out.

Awinita and Adahy began laughing. They didn't know which was funnier: the answer of catfish or the old sea-man's reaction.

"I have another one," Dustu offered. "What do you call a smelly sting ray?"

There was silence among the group, then the young sea-man said loudly, "A stink ray!"

Awinita and Dustu clapped their hands, "Yes! That's it. You got it!"

"You really did get it!" the dolphins laughed.

"I have another one!" Chipper gleefully twirled around in a circle. "What do you call a lazy lobster?"

There was silence again throughout the group. Then Marco said, "It seems that nobody knows that one. So, Chipper, what *do* you call a lazy lobster?"

"A *slob*ster!"

Even the grumpy old sea-man almost smiled.

Chapter 43

Water Spout

Much time had passed and the fairies long journey home was nearly at an end. They had crossed the great sea and would soon reach the shore. Everyone was tired, including the dolphins and Marco. Chipper had said goodbye weeks ago, because his home was on the side of the sea that they had left behind. The sea people also left them when the ark was safely out beyond any possible trouble from the Roman ships. They wished the fairies a safe journey and then returned to their undersea homes.

That evening after dinner, the fairies sat on the roof of the ark and watched the sun set. In the distance they could see strange things that extended from the dark clouds to the water. Adahy thought out to Marco and asked him what he thought they might be. He replied that they were water spouts, which were like tornados but in the water instead of on the land. The fairies watched as the water spouts appeared and then disappeared. After the sun set, they flew down off the roof and Marco called to them.

"Looks like a storm is coming," he thought to them. "You had better make sure everything is secure."

A bit fearful, Awinita asked, "How bad do you think it will be?"

"There's no way to tell for sure, except that it seems to be coming this way and the clouds are getting thicker and darker," Marco replied. "It might be a pretty big one."

"I sure hope not," she murmured, remembering the terrible storm that took Waya's life.

"We'll be just fine," Adahy tried to reassure her. "Look how far we have come. We'll be home before you know it."

Dustu looked anxiously back and forth between Adahy and Awinita. He hoped Adahy was right.

The three fairies quickly rushed about to see that everything was tightly closed or lashed down. They closed the windows and tightly latched them, but left one door open so that they could watch the sea. They didn't really need to watch the sea, because it quickly became obvious that they were in a storm. The boat began to rock back and forth, and the wind grew stronger. Then it began to rain—hard!

Adahy closed the door and then the three flew to their hammocks for safety. They waited. Marco called to them, "I'm going deeper because I cannot risk the boat slamming into me— and break apart. The dolphins are coming with me. We'll still be here; we won't go far. Try not to worry."

"Thanks, Marco," the three thought back to him.

Awinita leaned over and whispered to Adahy, "It's too late for that. I'm already worried."

Adahy smiled reassuringly to her, "After all we've been through, we can certainly handle this. We're so close to the shore we could almost fly home by ourselves."

"WHOA!" Dustu yelled out as the boat lurched and dipped. Their hammocks violently swung back and forth as they tightly hung on. Then the lightening started—one loud crash after another. Suddenly there was a deafening strike of lightening that shook the boat. Awinita screamed in terror!

"I think we were hit!" Adahy shouted as he flew from his hammock to the door. He opened it and smoke billowed inside. He saw bright flames against the wood railing. "We're on fire!"

Dustu and Awinita quickly flew to the door as Adahy began to shut it. They all started coughing from the smoke.

"What do we do?" Dustu choked out.

"Marco!" Adahy thought out to the great whale. "We're on fire!"

Marco immediately swam to the surface, and blew out a huge spray of water onto the ark, then immediately dove down again as he thought out to them, "I think it's out now. Check it and let me know ... but be careful. The waves are very rough."

Adahy opened the door. He held onto the door frame as he peered out. Between Marco and the rain, the flames were gone, but the smoke inside was still strong. Awinita and Adahy opened two windows to let the powerful wind blow the smoke out, then they securely latched them shut again.

The boat was pitching up and down and back and forth, getting more violent as the minutes passed. Then the ark began to spin around and around.

"I think we're in a water spout!" Adahy shouted.

"Uuhhh," Dustu moaned loudly. "I'm going to puke!"

Then he leaned over the hammock and did. "Booouuuh!" Poor Dustu retched. "Booouuuh!"

"It's OK, Dustu, don't worry about it. Just hold on!" Awinita reassured him.

The boat continued to swirl around.

"Oh no," Adahy groaned. "I'm going to throw up toooo ... Bwaaaak! Bwaaaak! Bwaaaak!" he heaved.

Awinita held her hand over her mouth but then she vomited just like the others.

The rain ferociously pounded the roof and deck. It got heavier and then it sounded like rocks were raining down.

"What is *that!*" Dustu shouted out in alarm.

"It sounds like hail!" Adahy yelled over the deafening pounding of hail smashing onto their boat.

Suddenly, with a great tearing sound, something crashed through the roof! A giant ice hailstone bounced off the floor and then slid across the room. Then another hole was torn through the roof! And then another! Rain and pieces of frozen hail poured through the holes. The fairies all screamed in terror.

"Here!" Adahy yelled. "Over here!" He swung off his hammock and ran to the corner of the walls. Awinita and Dustu scurried with him. They hunched down together as the ark was unmercifully pounded and pounded.

Suddenly all was calm. "What's going on?" Dustu exclaimed. "Is the storm over?"

"I don't know," Adahy said, wondering. He stood and walked to the nearest window and carefully opened it. "This is really strange," he said. "Right here the water is mostly calm, and the sun is shining, but just ahead it's very dark. I don't think we're clear yet." He re-latched the window and re-joined the others.

Adahy was right. The storm started up again, except that it was even more fierce. The fairies huddled together as the boat rose and fell, and twisted about by the terrible waves.

Suddenly they heard the panicked warning thoughts from the dolphins, "Rocks ahead! Rocks!"

Marco quickly lunged for the pulling straps. He caught them in his mouth and began to swim away from the rocky reef ahead. He fought the strong current that was forcing the boat toward the deadly sharp rocks. He thought toward the fairies, "Hang on!"

The fairies waited in fear as they felt the tug of the straps pulling their boat against the vicious waves.

Suddenly, the straps broke!

The ark lurched and the fairies were jolted from their corner and tumbled across the floor, screaming in terror. A great swell of water lifted the ark up and then violently down again. And again! The third time, there was a terrible grinding sound that sounded like a ferocious sea monster! The boat had been thrown up and onto the sharp rocks. The ark crashed to a stop on the jagged cold stones. The terrible jolt stunned the frightened fairies. They could hear water rushing into the bottom of their torn boat.

Horrified, Marco and the dolphins watched helplessly as the ark was dashed upon the sharp rocks and ripped apart.

"Don't be afraid!" Awinita loudly called out. "If we die, we go to see the Lord Jesus!"

"He won't let us die!" Adahy hollered back. "He won't! We have come all this way to bring back the stories about Him and to spread His words!"

Now the seawater was rushing across the floor. "To the hammocks!" Adahy called out. The three flew to their hammocks and watched the water flood in. The water continued to rise at an alarming rate. Then, with a great tearing sound, the front half of their boat ripped away! Nearly unbelieving, they stared out through the great ragged opening. As bright lightening flashed across the sky, they saw the terrifying dark and jagged rocks close in front of them.

More and more sea water flooded in. "We have to get on the roof!" Adahy yelled. He flew to one of the large holes that a hail stone had punched through. He flew out and turned. While holding tightly to the edge of the torn wood, he called to Awinita and Dustu, "Come on!"

213

They flew up and out of the hole. They all held on as the rain thoroughly soaked them. They anxiously looked about but could see nothing but rocks, wild waves, and darkness. They didn't even try to talk as the rain pelted them.

"Marco has an idea!" the thought voice of Finn called to them. "He says that the storm is going away, but you are still in danger. Fly down and hold onto our air-holes and we will take you to him."

Then Binka and Tinka's heads broke the rough surface of the water. Seeing them being lifted up and down with the waves, Adahy hesitated and then called to them, "Our wings are all wet, so we'll have difficulty flying!"

The three dolphins swam as close to the rough rocks as they dared. "You must! Come now!" Finn called to them.

"Let's go!" Adahy said firmly. "Be strong and have faith."

The three fairies shook their wings to get as much water off them as they could, and then rose clumsily up into the air. They barely made it to the waiting dolphins below. The dolphins immediately headed out and away from the rocks. Holding tightly to the dolphin's air opening on the top of their heads, the fairies could see the great dark shape of Marco ahead. The rain still pounded down upon them, but did seem to be lessening. Adahy turned to look back at their boat. He was just in time to see a great wave wash across it … and drag the battered remains of it off the rocks and down into the depths below.

The ark was now totally gone.

"Fly into my mouth!" Marco said as he opened his great maw.

The fairies were shocked. "What?"

"Fly into my mouth, I said," Marco repeated. "You'll be safe in here."

With no other options, other than drowning, the fairies did just that. They struggled to fly from the dolphin's heads and into Marco's great wide-open mouth.

Chapter 44

A Whale of a Tale

Marco swam up the shore-line and away from the storm.

"Marco! Please don't sneeze!" Dustu exclaimed anxiously. Then he added, "Or swallow!"

"Don't worry, my little friend," Marco chuckled. "This isn't the first time a whale has had someone in his mouth."

"Really?" Dustu asked, incredulously. "You do this a lot?"

"No, but I will tell you the story of Jonah. He was told by God to go to a wicked city and warn the people there to stop their evil ways. But Jonah didn't want to go, so he bought a ticket for travel on a ship to another place. God made a great storm on the sea. It was so bad that the ship was in danger of sinking, and the men on board prayed to all their false gods to calm the storm, but nothing happened. So they figured that one of their passengers, Jonah, might be the cause of the storm because he had disobeyed his God … the one true God. Jonah said for them to toss him overboard so that God would then calm the storm. So they did. And the storm was calmed.

Poor Jonah was tossed about in the waves and seaweed wrapped around him. He called out to the Lord and thanked Him for his salvation, even though he had sinned and was drowning. The Lord sent a whale and the whale swallowed Jonah right up! For three days and three nights, Jonah prayed from inside the whale. Then the Lord told the whale to vomit him up onto the land. Once again, the Lord told Jonah to go to the wicked city, and this time … he went!"

"I guess he did!" the fairies agreed.

Dustu thought for a moment, and then asked, "Do you think that God made the storm to crash our boat?"

"No, I doubt that," Marco replied. "Sometimes things happen. God has His reasons … reasons that we will never know." Then he chuckled, "Jonah was swallowed, but don't worry, I'm not going to swallow you!"

"Thanks," Adahy grinned. "We very much appreciate that."

"You are welcome," Marco replied, "But I do have one request. Try not to move about … because it tickles!"

*

The rain had stopped and the sun was coming out from behind the clouds. Marco opened his great mouth and the grateful fairies flew out. They landed on the waiting dolphins.

"Well, my little friends, this is the end of my part of this great journey," Marco thought gently.

"How can we possibly repay you?" Adahy said with heartfelt gratitude. "What you have done for us is beyond …"

Marco interrupted him, "I need no repayment of any sort. You should know this. It was my honor to assist you."

The three fairies looked into his great eye. "Thank you ever so much," Adahy said, as he bowed his head to Marco.

Awinita flew back over to Marco and knelt on his back. She bent down and kissed his smooth wet skin. She laid her cheek against him and whispered, "Thank you for your great kindness."

Then Dustu blinked back a tear as he said, "You are my biggest best friend in the whole world. I'll never forget you as long as I live."

"Goodbye, my friends," Marco thought to them as he quickly turned away and started to swim out into the ocean. He didn't want to know if a whale could cry.

The dolphins carried the three fairies toward the shore. When they got as close as they could, the fairies flew up off them and into the air. With love, they looked at the three dolphins. "You have been such good friends to us. You have traveled across the great sea and then back again for us. We cannot thank you enough," Adahy smiled.

"We will love you forever," Awinita said with tears in her eyes.

"I wish you could come with us," Dustu said sadly. "I wish you could be with my friends and me at our village."

"That sounds like fun, but impossible," Finn thought back.

"Yes, it does sound like fun," Binka added. "We will miss you."

"It has been an adventure for us to be with you," Tinka thought to them. "I could have done without the shark attack, but except for that, it was all fun. We hope you have a safe journey to your home."

The fairies waved goodbye to their dolphin friends as they swam away. The fairies watched for a few moments and then suddenly the three dolphins leapt high up out of the water and spun around! Then they splashed back into the sea, giggling.

"Show-offs!" Dustu grinned.

Chapter 45

Home

The three fairies sat on the sand and rested while the warm sun dried them. "We have nothing left," Awinita sighed. "No food, fresh water, nothing."

"Yeah, and no sweet dates," muttered Dustu.

"You're both wrong," Adahy said softly. "We have everything because we have each other. That's the most important thing of all."

Awinita smiled at Adahy, "You are so right. We do have each other, so let's stop feeling sorry for ourselves and get to work."

They heard the flutter of wings as two seagulls landed on the sand next to them.

"Hi there," one gull greeted. "Got any food?"

"No, we don't," Dustu frowned. "We …"

"Hey! I remember you!" the other gull exclaimed. "You were here before!"

"Yes, we were," Adahy thought to them. "Can you help us? Would you find an eagle and ask him to come and speak with us?"

The seagulls cocked their heads and stared at him. Adahy continued, "I'm sorry, we don't have anything to give you, but would you please help us anyway? We really need you."

The gulls put their heads together for a private conversation, and then one said, "Will the eagle give us food?"

"I don't know," Adahy answered. "Sorry."

"Hmmmm. Well, alright then," the gulls decided. "We'll help anyway."

"Thank you! Thank you!" the fairies called to the birds as they soared up into the air.

Soon three eagles appeared. They were surprised that the gulls had agreed to help the fairies without any promise of reward, so they complimented the generous seagulls ... and caught some fish for them anyway.

The eagles carried the fairies up the coast to a fresh-water river. There they turned inland and flew alongside the river. After a short while, the familiar smell of pine trees and earth replaced the salty air, reminding them that home was near. Soon the eagles landed in a clearing among the trees.

While Awinita weaved some bags with long grass, Adahy and Dustu gathered greens, nuts, and berries. Soon the friendly eagles returned with three deer who agreed to carry the fairies back to their home.

*

As they had promised before, they stopped by the village of the human people to tell them of Jesus. To their surprise, they found the village empty. The deer told them that sometimes the people would travel to other places for finding food, and then return again.

So, after deciding that one day they would return to the village, they continued onward toward home. When they were almost there, the animals of the forest ran or flew ahead to tell everyone that they were coming.

They had been gone for so many months. It was going to be wonderful to be back home again. The owl called out to the village, "They're here! They're here!"

Home! They had arrived! They thanked the deer for carrying them back to their village. As the deer disappeared into the forest, all of the village fairies rushed to greet them.

As soon as she heard the owl's call, Awinita and Dustu's mother excitedly flew to meet them. Overjoyed, she threw open her arms and hugged and kissed them. "You're back! You're back safe and sound! My goodness, look at you, Dustu. You've grown! You are almost a man! You'll be as tall as Waya before you know it!" She looked around, "Where is Waya?"

"He didn't make it, mom," Awinita whispered softly.

"Oh, no," her mother said with dismay, then she noticed Awinita's wing. "Oh! Your wing! It's healed!" she gasped, staring at it in wonder. "It's whole again!"

"We'll tell you all about it later," Awinita smiled as they began to walk toward their home.

"Hey, mom?" Dustu asked, "Is it time for lunch?"

His mom laughed as she kissed him on the top of his head, "Yes! Let's go get some lunch!"

*

Dustu's mother was amazed when Dustu cleaned his own dish after lunch. She was even more amazed when he went to gather firewood—without even being asked to! She smiled to herself as she watched him. He's so much more mature now than when he left.

Chapter 46

The Fairy Stone Cross

Later that evening, the feast began. Everyone was full of joy as they shared a huge wonderful meal together. After dinner, when the sun began to set, the village elder stood and addressed the people, "We are so blessed to have our friends back again after their long journey. Would you, Adahy and Awinita, please stand and tell us of what you have learned?"

"And Dustu, sir," Adahy reminded.

"Yes, of course, and Dustu," he said, smiling at the boy.

Together the three fairies took turns telling of their travel to the great sea, and of the people they met along the way. They told of the long sea voyage and of their friends Marco and the dolphins. They told of the beauty of the blue sea algae, and the peril of the storm. With great sadness, they told of brave Waya's death. They told of meeting their friends, the sea-people, and how they helped them avoid being caught by the Romans. They told of the man, kind Mr. Jericho.

The hours passed as they told of their travel with the caravan and the new friends they met along the way. They told of the stories they heard about Jesus: how He fed the crowds, how He healed the sick and the lame, how He made the blind see and the deaf hear, how He cast demons out, and how He even raised the dead to life again! The crowd was amazed at the miracles He performed, and they eagerly wanted to know more and more about Him.

The fairies laughed when Jesus cast the merchants out of the Holy Temple, but they fell silent when they were told of His arrest. The fairy people listened in horror as they were told of how Jesus was whipped and beaten. In anger, they leapt up from their seats on the grass when they were told of how Jesus was nailed to the cross, and how He hung there in awful pain. They yelled out, "No! How could that happen?"

Awinita's voice broke with emotional sadness and she could no longer talk. Adahy had to continue with the awful events as the story progressed to His death. Tears ran down Awinita's face as Adahy told how Jesus had asked forgiveness from God for those who were doing those terrible things to Him.

By now all the fairy people were standing with horror on their faces. "This is terrible! They killed Him!" they shouted as tears ran down their cheeks. "How could they kill the Son of God! How could they kill someone who did nothing but good!" They continued crying out as their tears flowed and dropped to the ground ... even the bravest and strongest men were weeping.

"Listen! Listen!" Adahy, Awinita, and Dustu called out loudly over all the crying fairies. "There's more! The best part! Please listen!"

Everyone calmed down and the fairies continued their story. "After three days dead in His tomb, Jesus came alive! He came alive!"

In abrupt silence, all the village fairies stared at Adahy, Awinita, and Dustu. The village elder then spoke, "He's alive? You saw Him?"

"Yes, we saw Him many times! And the last time we saw Him He rose up into heaven surrounded by the most beautiful cloud we have ever seen!"

The entire village began cheering and clapping! Suddenly, all across the ground, the night's darkness was filled with brilliant flashes of sparkling light! The dazzling lights grew larger and larger and then gently exploded! Each and every teardrop shed in sadness had miraculously transformed into a little stone cross!

The fairy people were stunned. They stared at the ground in amazement. Then each cautiously reached down and picked up a beautiful stone cross. "The Cross of Jesus!" someone shouted. Then all the people called out with joy! "He's here! He's here! It's a miracle! He has given us a gift!"

Adahy picked up a cross from the ground where Awinita tears had fallen. In awe, he handed it to her. She took it gingerly from his hand and carefully examined it. It was smooth and had a beveled shape. It was indeed a cross!

Awinita, Adahy, and Dustu joyously laughed and sang with their friends and family. After a while, they all sat down again, smiling and laughing as they marveled at their gifts from Jesus. Adahy continued their story by telling the happy group that Jesus had said that He would one day come back again. Hearing that, the fairy people clapped with joy!

* * *

It was a beautiful night. Awinita stood in the darkness outside her family's home and stared up at the brilliant stars above.

Adahy came up and stood next to her. "Why are you out here all by yourself? Is anything wrong?"

Awinita smiled at him and answered, "No, I'm just thinking."

"Just thinking about what?" he smiled down at her.

"All that has happened."

"Yes," Adahy agreed. "A lot has happened."

"I'm so grateful to Jesus for healing my wing, but I have a confession to make ... I've also missed your arms around me when you had to carry me everywhere."

"You mean like this?" Adahy grinned as he playfully put his arms around her.

"Yes," she murmured, "exactly like this."

Adahy smiled and then he whispered through her hair into her delicate ear, "Just remember, soon you'll be old enough to marry."

"No, Adahy," she pulled back slightly and looked up at him. "Now I *am* old enough to marry."

They both smiled at each other ... and then they kissed.

Legend of the
Fairy Stone Cross

"Long ago, in the land now known as Patrick County, Virginia, there lived happy fairies. One day, visitors arrived from a distant land and brought news of the death of Christ. When the fairies heard of His crucifixion, they wept and their tears fell to the ground. But when they heard of His Resurrection, their tears of sorrow turned into beautiful little crosses."

* * *

For many years people revered these little crosses in superstitious awe, in the belief that they protected the wearer against witchcraft, sickness, accidents and disaster.

Fairy stones are staurolite, a combination of silica, iron and aluminum. They are found from tiny ¼ inch to 2 inches long. Staurolite crystallizes at 60 or 90 degree angles, hence the stone's cross-like structure.

Found only in rocks once subjected to great heat and pressure, the mineral was formed long ago during the rise of the Appalachian Mountains. The stones are most commonly shaped like St. Andrew's cross, an "X," but the "T" shaped Roman crosses and square Maltese crosses are the most sought-after. The rare staurolite stones are found elsewhere in the world, but not in such abundance than at **Fairy Stone State Park**.

Fairy Stone State Park, located in Patrick County, Virginia, opened on June 15, 1936. The park's cross-shaped namesake stone is prevalent in the region, which also features beautiful scenery, rich history, and ample recreational opportunities. The park consists of 4,868 acres, making it the largest of the six original state parks, and still one of the largest to this day.

Please enjoy other books by C. C. Archambeault.

The **Star Man's Son** series:

Star Man's Son

Star Man's Son: Discovery

Star Man's Son: Rescue
(to be released late summer 2017)

And coming soon:

A Life of Miracles

Made in the USA
Middletown, DE
10 May 2017